WORLDS AWAY

WORLDS AWAY: BOOK ONE

JL HENDRICKS

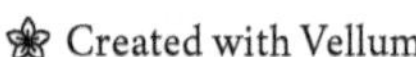

OTHER BOOKS BY J.L. HENDRICKS (MY 1ST PEN NAME)

New Orleans Magic

Book 1: New Orleans Magic

Book 2: Hurricane of Magic

Book 3: Council of Magic

Worlds Away Series

Book 0: Worlds Revealed (join my Newsletter to get this exclusive freebie)

Book 1: Worlds Away

Book 2: Worlds Collide

Book 2.5: Worlds Explode

Book 3: Worlds Entwined

A Shifter Christmas Romance Series

Book 0: Santa Meets Mrs. Claus

Book 1: Miss Claus and the Secret Santa

Book 2: Miss Claus under the Mistletoe

Book 3: Miss Claus and the Christmas Wedding

Book 4: Miss Claus and Her Polar Opposite

The FBI Dragon Chronicles

Book 1: A Ritual of Fire

Book 2: A Ritual of Death

Book 3: A Ritual of Conquest

Chronicles of the Unwanted Princess –

Published by LMBPN Publishing

Book 1: The Portal of Chance

Book 2: The Forbidden Portal

Book 3: The Emerald Portal

Mr. Claus Series coming Christmas 2021

See these titles and more at https://www.jlhendricksauthor.com/

The peal of the claxon bells could be heard all through the ship, and the crew rushed to and fro as they took their duty stations to prepare for the inevitable. "Rotna, get off the comm with your mate. NOW is the time to focus on the ship, not some female." the Commander yelled as he gave Rotna a stern frown and pointed to the weapons console.

Rotna usually manned the weapons console during battles. However, it has been a few years since this crew had seen any battles. All had been calm during these trips until this one.

"I must go now, stay safe and know that I love you!" Rotna ended his comm with his mate and focused back on the weapons console, but he was too late. A charged torpedo hit the side of the ship where Rotna was stationed. The console discharged an energy blast that threw him against the metallic desk that housed the science scanners behind him. His back hit the hard surface, and he fell to the ground unconscious.

"Someone get a medic here immediately! I need my weapons officer back on task." The Commander gave Rotna one more look and arched an eyebrow with the realization he wouldn't get his weapons officer back on duty any time soon. The ship warbled as another torpedo hit a different spot on the same side of the ship. All the warriors on the bridge looked to the Commander as he stumbled to the weapons console. At the same time his second in command, Eereen, made his way to the weapons station from across the bridge.

The Commander arrived first so he loaded and launched four torpedoes and sent them off one after the other in rapid fire towards the enemy ship that had attacked them. This enemy had supposedly agreed to a tentative truce some years back and would on occasion play chicken with the V'Zenian ships, but they never would have openly attacked like this. The Commander wondered what would have caused them to attack without provocation.

"Eereen, fire the laser cannons at will and target their port engine. Let's see if we can't damage their ship enough to keep them from firing any more torpedoes," the Commander yelled as he handed over the weapons con to his First Officer.

"Yes, Sir!" Eereen stated as he sat at the console. He quickly reviewed the ship in front of them and targeted the port side engines with both laser cannons and another round of torpedoes. He had to be careful since they did not have many left. This ship should not have seen any combat on this trip. It was only on a trip to Earth to pick up another load of slaves and possible mates for their species. In the four trips he has made, they never saw anything more than space dust in their path.

The Chief Engineer reported to the Commander, "Sir, that last set of torpedoes damaged our engines along with the artificial gravity generator. I sent technicians to fix them, but I can't guarantee that parts of the ship will have enough gravity to function properly."

He pushed the green button on his console. "Listen up,

this is the Commander. We have an issue with our gravity generator and certain areas could intermittently lose artificial gravity. Use the hand rails if you must move about the ship, otherwise strap in and prepare for a bumpy flight." The Commander knew that his slaves in the holding cells had nothing to help them stay secure. He briefly wondered if he shouldn't release their cell doors so they could at least find some seats to strap themselves into. But before he could think of it anymore, another round of torpedoes made their way past the energy shield his ship had up.

"Someone tell me how those torpedoes are making their way past our shields! They should not have access to such technology! I want a solution before they blow us out of the universe! And I want something that will destroy them- five minutes ago!" The Commander sat down and strapped himself into his command chair. Then reviewed the schematics they had of the enemy ship based on their scans over the past twelve hours.

The slaves in the holding cells had bumped around and most had nothing more severe than contusions. A few broke some bones and had cried out for help, but all of the guards who had been in their holding areas, had left before the battle began.

"Hey, listen up! Grab ahold of the bars and wrap yourselves around them as best you can. This is worse than a 'bumpy flight,'" one man yelled out to everyone.

The ship kept taking hits from torpedoes and laser cannons, and it jumped and jostled. When the gravity generator in the section housing the slaves died, most had already wrapped themselves around the bars. However, a few did not, they sat on the ground and held onto each other and tried to wait out the ride.

This proved to be a fatal mistake. Three of the human slaves who had not held on tightly to the bars flew around like a cow in a tornado, hit their heads and died immediately.

One had her head twisted so far back that she looked more like a rag doll thrown to the ground. The other two women continued to bump around their cell and hit the other women who were trying to hold on for their lives.

"Oh please God, if you can hear me, help me to survive this, and I will do whatever you want me to do for the rest of my life. Even if that means I have to marry one of these alien freaks, I will do it." One human woman, Natalie, prayed as she closed her eyes and tried not to think about the horrible ways she might die on this ship.

1

JENNA

One week earlier

One minute I was checking out a nice-looking man across the field, the next I was in his arms inside of some strange metallic room. "Wha…who are you? Where am I?" I whispered as my head spun.

The man who held me looked into my face and his eyes widened. "Oh nuts! How are you awake already? I just transported you from Earth. You should have been out for hours."

I realized I was in his arms, which were as huge and firm as a cannon, no joke. "Hey big guns, you wanna let me down?" I looked into his violet eyes and was momentarily mesmerized by the most beautiful face I had ever laid eyes on. This man had to be pushing seven feet tall, with long, wavy, dark hair that went to his shoulders and a strong chiseled face. His clothes looked like something anyone would wear on the beach, tan board shorts and a conservative Hawaiian print shirt with surf boards on it.

"I am not carrying any guns." He had this perplexed look

on his face, like he didn't understand the name I had given him.

"Dude, let me down! NOW!" I took my one free arm and banged it on his chest in hopes that he would get my meaning. Instead, my hand ached from hitting something as hard as concrete. There was a tingling sensation going throughout my hand, so I shook it out in hopes of that feeling dissipating faster, "Ow!"

He set me down and took one step back. "I won't hurt you." Then he took one step closer and lightly brushed the hair away that had fallen into my face. His touch sent chills down my back as I gasped from the connection I felt with him.

In a whisper I asked him, "Who are you?" Then I took a step away from him. He was too close for me to breathe properly.

"I am Commander Venay of the V'Zenian Empire. You are on my star cruiser, *The Zamaya*." He looked down at me with something akin to pride in his eyes. I got the feeling that he was proud of his title, or maybe his ship.

I looked around at my surroundings and tried to process what he just said, but a headache was developing. "Are you punking me?" There was an ache behind one eye, and I closed it and tried to rub my eyelid while breathing heavily.

"What is 'punking'?" He tilted his head slightly while looking at me with narrowed eyes, and then he scratched the back of his head.

"This is some sort of joke, right? I mean the last thing I remember is seeing you from across the field and then waking up in your arms here. Something isn't adding up. There's no way we're in space right now or even on a spaceship…" I looked around with pursed lips and tried to rub the goosebumps from my arms.

"Did you drug me and take me to some sort of sound stage? I didn't sign up to be on a reality show or anything like that. So if this is some sort of TV or movie production, you have the wrong person." I slowly moved away from the giant and walked around the room. We were standing on a metallic floor, and the room was small, maybe a ten by ten square room. On one wall was what looked like a door, but it didn't open out; there appeared to be no way for it to open. I could see the lines of the door, but no hinge. There was one medium sized, circular window. Outside, they had done a great job of making it look like I was in space.

We must have been facing out towards space because I couldn't see Earth or even the moon. The view was filled with stars as far as I could see. One small speck looked like it could be a planet, as it was bigger than all of the other stars around us, but I couldn't be sure. The room was pretty cold, so they were doing a great job of simulating outer space with environment as well as with the view. The room had a clean scent, like fresh laundy.

I looked back at the man who had taken me, and he was smiling. What was that about?

"Do you believe me now? That planet you can see is actually what you humans call Jupiter." He looked out the window, and I took the opportunity to get a better look at him. His skin color wasn't different from mine, but he did have some weird colored veins going up his arm. I could believe the veins were sticking out, just like any huge muscular guy's arms. But the color had me perplexed. The veins pulsed and changed colors. One moment it was pulsing in a blueish tint, then the next it was pink, then orange.

What kinda show was this?

"Um, I think you have done a great job with the special effects outside this room. But I don't believe that we are in space." I walked over toward what appeared to be the door and pushed on it, nothing happened. "How do I open this door?"

Venay walked up behind me and ran his hand over something on the side of the door, and it swished open, just like in the movies. The door moved sideways into the wall, and what I saw on the other side of the door freaked me out. There were more people, but they were in cages.

I gasped and covered my mouth with my hand before any sounds of horror could escape.

Surrounding them were guards of some sort that looked similar to my captor, but they all were wearing some type of military uniform. The uniforms were tight fitting, button up shirts with a rank of some sort on the collars, not too different from an Army uniform. The pants were black cargo style, and they had a weapons belt with a dagger on one side and what appeared to be a toy phaser gun on the other.

I started to walk out into the room, but he put his arm around my waist and brought me back inside as the door slid shut.

"What are you doing? I want to go home! NOW!" I turned into him since he hadn't let go of my waist yet and tilted my head up to look into his face.

He looked down at me and with a smug look and said, "It isn't safe for you to go out there, unless you want to end up in a cage with the other humans?" Then he arched one eyebrow.

"Look, I don't know what's going on here, but I did *not* sign up for this, and I want to go home. Would you please stop playing these games and let me out of here?" I put my hands on his chest and tried to push myself away from him, but he held on tight.

"Human, tell me your name. Unless you want me to keep calling you Human?" He used his free hand to move my long auburn hair so that it fell along my back. Then he ran his hand through it. I had goosebumps again, but this time it wasn't because I was cold. In fact, it was just the opposite. There seemed to be some sort of supernatural attraction. I didn't want to be attracted to him, but I was. His pulsing veins were calling my name and asking me to kiss them, maybe even nibble on those along his neck. Sweat was starting to form on my brow as this man held me.

As soon as I came back to my senses, I moved my shoulders in an effort to get his hand out of my hair.

"Paris, my name is Paris. Can you please let me go now?" I couldn't look into his eyes any longer. He was doing something to me with those hypnotic eyes of his. Instead, I focused on those cannons for biceps and watched as his veins pulsed out different colors, but the purple color seemed more dominant than the rest.

"You are named after a city in France? Why?" He looked down at me with that perplexed look of his again, and then let me go. I walked back towards the wall and took a deep breath.

"Wait, how do you know about the city in France?"

"The last group of slaves I picked up came from there. Not too many of them spoke English, but our Universal Translator worked just fine with them. Well, until they tried taking it out of their head." He chuckled at that moment and had a far off look on his face, as though he was remembering something funny.

"One of them swore we were conducting human experiments on them and that the sub-dermal translator we installed into the side of the skull, near their ear, was an alien listening device." Again, he laughed at the memory, while motioning with his arms out wide. "Where do you humans come up with this stuff? I mean, really, an alien listening device?" He shook his head as he continued to laugh.

"If we wanted to listen in on your conversations, we have much better devices for that." His smile helped to soften the hard lines on his face.

"It doesn't feel like you have implanted anything into my skull." I moved my hands around my head feeling for anything out of place and found nothing wrong.

"Because I haven't - not yet anyway. During the trip, we examine and perform the implantation so that all of you can understand us before we arrive to your new home. All of the guards and soldiers on this ship speak English so there shouldn't be any linguistic issues until we get home." The alien Commander took a few steps toward the wall, giving me a good look outside of the window again.

"Does that mean that all of your prisoners are from North America?" I wondered how many people they had kidnapped and what was really going on here.

He thought for a moment, "Hm, I believe so. We picked up a few in Japan, but they were speaking English before we picked them up. We do try to keep similar languages on each trip. It's much easier that way for the crew to interact with you humans until the translators are installed."

I thought about his earlier question and decided I might as well answer him. Maybe he would let me go if he thought I was a real person. Isn't that what they teach you to do if you are ever kidnapped? Make the assailant view you as a real human being and hope they decided to release you, or at the very least not hurt you. But does that work if they are crazy? Cuz this guy was certifiably nuts!

I looked at him and gave him my best smile, "My parents wanted to honeymoon in Paris, but they couldn't afford it. However, they were happy to honeymoon in Vegas, where I was conceived. Instead of naming me Vegas, they decided to name me for the place of their dreams. Mom always said that she loved me more than Paris, which was kinda funny when I was a kid." I looked down and stopped smiling when I remembered what happened to them.

"That's a pretty story. I like your name." He walked over to a different wall and pushed a button I hadn't noticed before. The wall opened up and a sofa slid out before the wall closed. He motioned for me to sit down, and then he sat next to me. He was a bit too close for my comfort.

"Alright Venay, tell me what is really going on and where I am." I sat straight and on the edge of the sofa. My leg bounced up and down as I waited for his story.

"I might not look like it, but I am not from Earth, and we are on a spaceship heading to my home planet to be precise." He put his arm along the back of the couch.

"Um, I hate to break it to you, but we aren't moving. Did your special effects equipment breakdown or something?" I giggled at my stupid joke, but there was no way I was falling for this lame story of his.

"Of course we haven't left yet. We still have a shipment of slaves we are waiting for." He shook his head like he couldn't believe what I said.

"What do you mean slaves? Slavery was abolished a very long time ago and is illegal all over the world." Who was this guy to joke about something like that? Slavery wasn't a joking matter. But something in the back of my head was starting to warn me. What I had seen and heard was beginning to sound like it could be real.

"Human slaves are very real on my planet. I make one trip a year here to pick up a ship full of them to bring back. However, some are lucky enough to become mates to my species, if they so choose." He stopped talking and started checking out my body, and his eyes spent too much time on my chest for my liking.

"Hey, alien boy, up here." I pointed to my face, "My eyes are up here in case you were wondering. You know, since you're an alien you might not understand human anatomy." *Hmph men are all the same no matter where they come from.*

"Oh, I understand human anatomy just fine. My mother is human. That is why I look so similar to you." He stood up and turned around, so I could admire his fine *assets*, which only made my body hum and feel all tingly inside.

"Then what is your father?" He was taking this story pretty far, but sadly I was starting to believe him. This belief caused my heart to speed up and my head to feel foggy. I hoped I wasn't going to pass out.

We were interrupted by a communication in some foreign language that was quite guttural. I had no clue what they were speaking, maybe Klingon? He stood up and turned toward me.

"Paris, you might want to watch this." He put his hand out for me to take. I hesitated, wondering what he was up to. "You are safe with me; I promise you will not be harmed." He put his hand out again, and I took it. Venay pulled me up, and we walked to the one window in the room. He still held my hand. With his body so close to mine, I wanted him to do more than just hold my hand. My stupid body was aching to have him hold me in his embrace again. *What is wrong with me? This guy is crazy, and I want him to hold me?*

He kept a hold of my hand and motioned for me to look out the multi-paned window. "Wow, are we really moving? It doesn't feel like it." The stars outside were slowly moving and that planet looked as though we were approaching it. It didn't feel like we were moving, more like a 3D ride where we were stationary and everything around us was moving. Then I felt it, gravity began to shift, as did my reality. I felt heavier for a moment and almost fell over, but Venay let go of my hand and stood behind me with his arms wrapped around me, just like I wanted a few moments earlier.

This feeling was strange, my head was spinning, and my eyesight was a bit blurred. I think the cause was two-fold; blurry eyesight was from the movement in *space*, and the head spinning was from him being so near me. "What is this, one of those 4D rides at an amusement park? I know we are not in space. It's impossible."

An intoxicating scent enveloped my senses and my legs began to shake. The man holding me had a spicy scent mixed with an all male smell that had my olfactory nerve working overtime.

"Paris, it is very possible. Technically, I am part of a superior species that has had the ability to travel through space for well over 200 Earth years." He whispered in my ear, which just served to send a shiver down my spine. It was either excitement or fear, or maybe both. The idea that his species had been abducting people from my planet for two centuries was very frightening, but at the same time I couldn't quite believe it.

CHAPTER TWO

"Oh stink, this is real isn't it?" I started to slink down on the floor as my body began to register the movement in space and my eyes confirmed what I was feeling. All my senses were on overdrive, I could even taste the oxygen that had been pumped into the room. It almost felt like I was drowning.

Venay reached down and picked me up. He held me to his side while walking me back to the couch. "Are you ok? Is the oxygen mixture too high for you?" He was looking me over and paying close attention to my chest, but in this case I believed he was watching me take shallow breaths.

"Why can I taste the air? I shouldn't be able to do that." I looked at him with a raised eyebrow while breathing in deep.

"We have an increased level of oxygen when we first leave orbit around your planet. Over the years we have discovered that humans tend to pass out easily unless we do this. Your bodies have a difficult time processing oxygen while in shock as we leave your solar system. But once we get moving your bodies adjust. They really are quite adaptable to most environments. Another reason our ancestors chose your people to integrate with us." He puffed up his chest and sat up straighter. It looked like he took great pride in the fact that his ancestors abducted and experimented on humans.

His reaction only served to make me angry. I certainly wasn't impressed with his knowledge of our anatomy and physiology. "How could you take pride in the fact that your species has been kidnapping my people for two centuries? What do you do with my people? Do you force yourselves on the women? Force the men to be your slaves and do your hard labor?" I fisted my hands at my side and debated if I should hit him or try to run again. Although, I knew running wasn't an option at this point. It was at this point that I truly believed he was an alien and I was in space. Not sure how this all happened, but there it was.

He didn't answer me at first, he looked back towards the window and watched space as we hurtled through it. I had to admit, it was quite beautiful and oddly enough, calming. I felt myself relaxing and let go of my fisted hands and my shoulders started to loosen up as well.

"Paris, I will admit, our ancestors were not the most civilized. But we are very different now. We never force a woman to mate with us. If we take a human mate, she is very willing..." He looked at me and his eyes dilated while he gave me a smoldering smile.

"Hey now, don't go getting any ideas about me. I am NOT to be used as a breeding mare. No one who abducts me will be using me as a slave either. Stockholm Syndrome won't be my downfall." I got up and walked over to the window and sighed as I watched the stars zoom past. I put my arm on the side of the windowpane and leaned into it and whispered, "I will find my way home again."

"I chose you because you are my mate. I could feel it across the field when our eyes met. You felt it too, I know you did. The connection was visible on your face and when I touched you a moment ago as well."

"What exactly do you mean by *mate?*" I turned around and narrowed my eyes at the big alien.

"You would call it marriage. When we mate, it is with our one true love. The universe has created someone for all of us to love and join with. When we meet that *one*, we feel an instant sense of right, of belonging to each other. It is how my species have chosen their true mates since the beginning of time. There are exceptions, there are always those who can't wait and will sometimes mate with someone they were never meant to mate with and that always causes problems." He shook his head.

"You might as well lock me up with the other slaves, because no one is going to mate with me." I locked eyes with him and stared at him until he spoke again.

"If that is what you wish, but I must warn you. Without my protection, any of the males on this ship have the right to try and persuade you to become their mate." I tried to interrupt but he held up his hands, "They will not force themselves upon you or any other female, but they will try to get your attention in other ways… Most of the males who volunteer for this mission are looking for their mates. About half of the women will become mated to the men on this ship before we even reach our home planet." He stood up and walked to the door but stopped before opening it.

"Are you certain you would not reconsider and become my mate? I hold a very high rank and your life would be quite comfortable. You would be well taken care of and would want for nothing in life." He looked me over slowly as I thought on his words.

"I'm positive. There is no way on God's green Earth I would choose to give myself to anyone who kidnapped me. I want to go home and forget about this entire experience." I huffed out and put my arms around myself in an effort to comfort me. It didn't help.

"Paris, this is the last time I will offer you my protection.

You are intended to be my mate, I feel it. Life as a slave is not one you will enjoy. While we do treat our slaves better than we used to, it is still a very difficult life. One you will experience on this voyage home if you turn me down." He reached over and took a strand of my hair into his hands and slowly drew it between his thumb and forefinger.

I pulled my hair back and tried very hard to stop the shivers from going down my spine. That was too intimate of a gesture to accept from my abductor. "I'm positive. It would be preferable to rot away as a slave than to be used up as someone's mate."

He sighed and lowered his head for a moment, then stood up tall. Man was he tall, and imposing when he put his warrior mask back on. "Very well, but don't come to me when you find that you don't have enough food or warmth on this trip." He proceeded to open the door and he grabbed my arm rather forcefully and hauled me over to one of the cages in the other room.

"Open cage A-1, process this slave but make sure she gets extra in her evening meal." He took one last look at me and then walked away as another alien took me by the arm. I heard Venay say something about putting his uniform on and then he would be on the bridge.

CHAPTER THREE

As I watched Venay walk away from me, it saddened me that he didn't even look back at me once before he left the room. My heart was hurting, but I couldn't understand why, unless Stockholm Syndrome was already taking effect. I turned around and for the first time noticed how many men and women were in this room.

I let out a low whistle as I counted them. There must have been over 100 people crammed into cages that should have held half as many. Then I made the mistake of looking up into the face of my current captor. He was looking at me with a sneer on his face, "I don't know what the Commander saw in you, you are a scrawny thing who would not be able to give birth to a strong warrior of our race."

He opened up the closest cell and threw me in. "If you are going to make it on our planet, you will need to fatten up and build some muscles. No warrior in his right mind would choose you to mate with. You could only be good for domestic duties. I doubt we will get many offers for you as a slave either." As he walked away he said, "What a waste of space."

I didn't care what he said, and the fact that not many

would want me was even better. There was a chance I might make it back home after all. All I had to do was survive the trip and find a way back onto a ship going to Earth to abduct more humans, and I could get home and warn my planet about these aliens. That was what was most important. Not looking at those smoldering violet eyes again. Nope, not going to think about them, or the man those eyes belong to.

That warrior wasn't too far off when it came to how I looked. I had been living on the street since, well since that fateful night five years ago. I didn't talk about it much, but since I became homeless, my body had gone through a lot of changes. What muscle I did have was gone, along with at least thirty pounds, but I couldn't be certain. The last time I was in front of a mirror, I could see my rib cage poking through my skin. My eyes had permanent bags under them from lack of nutrition as well as sleep, and my nails… well, let's just say that my old manicurist would pitch a fit if she saw me now. But I didn't dwell on what was once my life.

Now I was a 22 year-old, young adult who found a way to live on the streets, safely. Not an easy feat, considering how many women didn't make it. I had always been able to take care of myself, and these past five years showed it. It wasn't as though men left me alone, at least not at first. They did try things, but I always fought them off, and they usually ended up more hurt than I did. In high school we were offered self-defense courses in PE, and my parents insisted I take them every year. I am truly thankful that they never gave in to my complaints.

The first year, I would come home from school sore and extremely tired every day. These classes were only offered during the last period of the day. Until I was able to get a driver's license and car, I had to endure the bus ride home while I was stinky and sweaty. At the time, I had no idea how beneficial those classes were going to be to my future survival.

Now on this ship, I had to make sure I could eat better and gain some muscle mass to ensure I could return to Earth. I still didn't know how I was going to do that, but first things first, I needed to gain weight.

My cell contained ten women. They were all in various shapes and sizes as well as skin color. Interesting, these aliens didn't seem to discriminate. Most were quite pretty, but a few looked like they were not picked to be mates, but more for manual labor. The woman closest to me had to be at least six feet tall and over 200 pounds of pure muscle. Her red hair was long but pulled back into a ponytail. She was wearing yoga pants, a t-shirt, and a matching zip up hoodie. "Hi, my name is Paris." I reached out to shake her hand.

She took mine in a firm grip that bordered on painful, "Hi there, I'm Sheila. Why did that alien have you in the other room? He didn't hurt you did he?" She raised her eyebrows while looking me over to see if I had any cuts or abrasions.

"No, thankfully." I shivered again thinking about how he did touch me. "He offered me a chance to be his mate, but I turned him down. I want nothing more than to get back home."

I looked over to the other women in our cell. "Do you have any idea what's going on here?" We were packed in pretty tightly. There was enough room for us all to sit down but not enough for us to lie down. When it came time for sleep, we were going to have a difficult time.

"I was going to ask you if you knew anything. All I can tell is that we have been taken by a group of aliens who look a lot like us. But that's all I know. There are more women than men, maybe 75% women? But I don't know if there is another room full or not." She gestured to the girl next to her. "This is Betsy, and she's barely 18. What do they want with kids? She hasn't even finished high school yet! And here she is, abducted by aliens." She shook her head.

I reached out to shake Betsy's hand, and she timidly

shook mine back in return. "Hi Betsy, don't worry, I don't think they're going to hurt us. But you should be prepared to be sold as a slave." I didn't want to tell her that most of the women here would be approached to become mates to these slave drivers. She seemed so young, I hoped they let her grow up a bit more. Even though she was of legal age, it was hard to imagine her with one of these aliens. I shuddered just thinking about that scenario.

Betsy started to cry and put her hands up over her eyes.

"What did you go and do that for?" Sheila glared at me, put her arm around Betsy, and tried to console her.

I stood up and looked at each and every girl or woman in my cell, "Listen up, I spoke with the Commander, the man who runs this ship. His crew have abducted us all and are taking us to their planet. We will most likely be sold as slaves." At that point the women in other cells started listening to me as well, and I could hear them murmur and some start to cry.

"I know this sucks. Trust me I am right there with you. But we have to be strong. We can't let them scare us or intimidate us. The Commander did say that none of his warriors would harm us. Well, if you can call kidnapping and selling us on the slave market not harming us." I gave a quick grunt and looked down at my feet while running my hand through my hair.

"There is another option here, if you are strong enough to try." I put a steely look on my face and gazed into all of their eyes as they watched me closely. "We could try to break out, take this ship from them, and turn it around. We would need to keep a few of them alive so we can force them to fly the thing, but I bet there are more of us than there are of them. What do you say? Are you with me?"

One of the warriors watching me from the other side of the room came over. I truly believed he couldn't hear me since I was just trying to speak to those in my cell and maybe the ladies in the cell next to mine. "Human, you won't be able to overpower us. But you were right, we won't harm you as long as you cooperate." Then he slowly looked over a couple of the woman and his gaze landed on one of the young women in the cage next to mine, "Or you could agree to be our mates. You have two options here, and her option," he pointed to me, "Isn't one of them". He licked his lips as he watched the young woman in the cage next to me squirm. "Hey, what's your name?"

The object of his attention fidgeted and looked at me and then over to him. He wasn't a bad looking guy, but they did just kidnap us all and were taking us to be slaves on another planet, so I could understand her hesitancy. She responded via a barely understandable whisper, "Natalie, but I have a fiancé back home so I am not interested in your proposition." She lowered her eyes down to the ground, and I could see tears coming from the side of her face.

The warrior laughed and walked back to his post, but he looked back over his shoulder and said, "We shall see about that." Then stood at his post and kept eyeing us all, but most of his attention was kept on Natalie.

"Hey, Natalie," Sheila whispered. "You might want to think about taking up his offer. If you mate with the dude he will keep you from being a slave. Who knows what those slave owners might do to us. Besides, he's not bad looking." She kept eyeing the warrior like he was her next meal. Sheila was one brave woman, or else just plain crazy.

She was taking this better than anyone so far. Most of the women I could see were either crying, or looking off into space. Not literally, of course. There were no portholes or windows in this room.

"How are you taking this so calmly? Have you been here a while and had time to process it all already?" She seemed like she was ok with all of this. How could anyone be ok with any of it?

"Because, I have always had a fascination with aliens. I go to the conventions, even the big one in Roswell. For me, this is like winning the lottery and realizing the money comes with a nice selection of cabana boys too." She suggestively raised her eyebrows and smiled while rubbing her hands together.

"Sheila, would you really consider becoming a mate instead of trying to get back home?" My jaw dropped, as I stared at her with wide eyes, and shook my hands while wishing they were around her neck.

"Oh yeah, have you seen them? They are *hot*. Besides, I have a feeling there are a lot more of them than we think. If they have been doing this for a while, they'll know how to handle us." She licked her lips as she checked out the three different warriors who stood guard inside our jail house.

I looked her up and down and considered her statement, "Hmm, you might be right." I slumped back down on the ground and ran both my hands through my hair and sighed. "How are we going to get home if we can't overpower them?" I looked up to her, almost resigned to being a slave for the foreseeable future. There was no way I would live out the rest of my life this way.

"Patience Paris, we play their game and hopefully things won't be so bad on their planet. Maybe we can even get a ride back to Earth someday soon." She looked back at our jailers and smiled at one of them. "I don't know how long this trip is. Do you?" She looked back down at me with furrowed brows.

"All I know is what Venay told me, and he said that we could become slaves or mates. It was a long trip to his planet and most of the women here would become mates before we made it to their home." I sighed and looked up at the ceiling, which was weird. It had diamond shapes carved into the material they had used to create the ceiling. It looked like metal of some sort, but I couldn't be sure since it was very shiny and glittered. It almost looked like the ceiling was made from diamonds the way it shone. I moved my head around and the light from the fixtures on the walls seemed to dance around the peaks of the imitation gems.

"On a first name basis with the Commander, huh? Are you sure you don't want to mate with him?" Sheila laughed at me, but Natalie gave us both a tear-filled, evil eye.

I narrowed one eye and pursed my lips, "Not a chance! I want to go home. Life wasn't the best, but I had a pretty good setup on the beach, and I miss my dog, Lola. I have no idea who will feed her now that I'm gone." I hung my head as I thought about Lola.

"Hey, I'm sure your family or friends will take care of Lola for you until you get home." Natalie tried smiling but she was still wiping tears away from her face.

"Nope, they won't." I didn't want to go into details, but just thinking about what I had lost made my heart ache. Even though it was a phantom pain, I still rubbed the area over my heart.

I needed to change the subject before anyone got too nosey. "So what are we going to do? Fall in line and mate with our abductors? Allow them to sell us into slavery? Or find a way to get home?" I whispered the last part, hoping the aliens couldn't hear me. But it seemed as though they did. What, were they descended from Superman or something?

Another warrior came over, "Hey, I know this has to suck for you, but there is light at the end of the tunnel. The journey will take almost five Earth months." He walked away laughing and then looked into another cell, "One of you just might fancy me before we get home." He raised his eyebrows up repeatedly as he checked out one of the other women in another cell. She stood up and walked to the bars closest to him and looked him up and down.

All of the women in the room, and even the human men, were deathly quiet as she whispered to the alien warrior. I couldn't hear anything, but I saw her smile at him. He walked closer to her and opened the door. She walked out and right into his arms. He kissed her right there in front of us all, and she kissed him back, quite eagerly too. The room went from total silence to hisses and cat calls.

The guy put her back in her cell, and she yelled, "What the heck! I thought we had the option to mate with you guys?" He locked the cell and smiled at her.

"I am still on duty. I can't take you back to my quarters until I am relieved." He looked her up and down. "What is your name?" He still smiled at her and reached for her hand through the cell.

As she let him take her hand, she said, "Lisa... what's yours?"

He kissed her hand, "Nice to meet you Lisa. I am called Rotna. After tonight, you will spend the rest of the trip in my quarters. They are much nicer than these cells." He looked around to the other women and said, "If any of you are as smart as my new mate, Lisa, you will allow the warriors to claim you. Your living conditions will be vastly improved as well as your meals. And once we are home, you will have the chance to earn the ability to roam around our world freely, as our mates. No one will harm you once you are mated. It is against our laws to touch another warrior's mate. You will live a good life with us. It is time to forget about your old life and look forward to the new and exciting life of a warrior's mate." He winked at Lisa and walked back to his post.

"But, if you choose to be a slave, be prepared to live a very hard life. One where you will work the equivalent of twelve to fourteen Earth hours a day and six days a week. Our time is measured a bit differently than yours on Earth. Our human slaves have told us that a V'Zenian day is about 1.5 hours longer than an Earth day. But we do have 7 day weeks. You will have one day off per week, if your master allows it. Slaves never have enough food or decent clothing. Your life will be difficult, and you may never be allowed to mate with a human male." He looked over to the males in the cages on the other side of the room and shook his head. He mumbled something, but I couldn't hear it.

"Sheila, did you hear what he said to the guys?" I really wanted to know, it could be important.

"Nah, I didn't hear him. But he does seem somewhat nice. I think we should pay close attention to Lisa and what happens to her. If she is treated well, I think I'm going to try and nab me a nice big alien hunk of meat!" She giggled as she eyed the other warrior who hadn't spoken to us since I entered the room. She started flipping her ponytail and smacking her lips. She was pulling out all of the stops to get his attention. But he wasn't buying it.

Later that night, I was given an extra portion of what they considered protein for my evening meal. I looked down at the plate in my lap. I guess Venay was making good on his word, he told me I would be taken well care of, and then told the guard to make sure I got a good evening meal. Not sure if this stuff is good, but at least I had a larger portion.

I sighed and used my fork to pick at what looked like a chalky jello mold, and it tasted pretty much like it looked. This was going to be difficult. But at least it was nutritious, or at least that is what they told us. If I could just get some muscle on I might be able to find a way to get back home. The only way to get home would be to fight, so I was going to have to get back in shape again. I realized that Sheila could help me too, she looked to be the kind who worked out a lot.

As much as I didn't want to, I started to think I might need to consider using Venay as a way to get back to Earth. If he was the one who always captained the ships that went to Earth and abducted women, maybe I could go with him as his mate on the next voyage. The idea that I would give myself to him as his mate just to get home wasn't pleasant, but maybe I could stall the whole mating stuff until later.

That might give me enough time to get back home, untouched. I was a virgin and had no plans to give that away to anyone except for my future husband. I had saved myself this long; what was another couple of years?

My high school boyfriend wasn't too happy with waiting. If my senior year had ended differently, then I might have given it to him. As it was, well… best not to dwell on what happened and what might have happened. Life turned out very differently for me than I ever thought it could.

CHAPTER FOUR

The next morning, or what we thought was morning, came too soon. The warriors turned down the lights and told us to go to sleep a couple of hours after we finished what passed as a meal, but if the noise level was anything to go off of, not many slept. I heard plenty of people crying and talking. Some were just whispering about the people back home they missed, others were trying to come up with a plan to escape. None of us could come up with anything good. These aliens were all taller and stronger than any of us. I finally realized why they picked us; none of us had combat experience. Sure, some had taken some self-defense classes, like me, but none of us had the kind of knowledge or experience we were going to need.

Sheila was doing some sort of exercise or stretching regimen that fit inside this tiny cell that caught my attention. "Hey Sheila, can you show me what you're doing? I think I'm going to need to get in better shape and fast."

She looked me up and down, taking in my size and body type. She scratched the back of her head while seeming to examine me. "Yeah, I think I can work with you. Don't know if you knew this, but I'm a personal trainer back home. I think I could help get you into shape if what they said was true. But it will take the entire five months of travel to do it, and you will have to do everything I tell you to do. No wimping out either." She started to play with her ponytail. Her hair was long, past the middle of her back, and red. Not the kind from a bottle either. It was a natural red with some lighter highlights. Her body looked like that of a body-builder; she had huge muscles all over. But it all made her look a bit like a man instead of a woman. I took a closer look at her and realized that she would have been really pretty if she was just a bit softer. But I guessed that some men prob-ably liked their women tough. These warriors would prob-ably like her, a lot.

"Whatever you say, I will do. I'm serious about getting back into shape. A few years ago I was very healthy and would have been considered fit. But living on the streets will change your body." I momentarily thought back to the way I looked when I was in high school and sighed. I was tall, about five feet eight inches. Well, tall for a human girl. I had longer auburn hair that had a very silky sheen to it. My hair-dresser used to tell me all the time how lucky I was to have such beautiful hair. Living on the streets tends to ruin most everything. Now my hair was dull and frizzy from not taking care of it. What I wouldn't give for a bottle of my old shampoo and conditioner again.

"The streets huh? I guess that's why you keep talking about fighting back. Did you have to fight back a lot? I mean, did umm…" Sheila was getting antsy, she kept bouncing back and forth between her feet and wouldn't look at me. She even rubbed the back of her neck as her face twisted with worry. I knew what she was thinking.

"I was fine. There were a few times where it got a bit dicey, but I was always able to fight my way out of it. Thank-fully I had taken self-defense classes in PE the entire time I was in high school. I have some pretty mad skills, but I need more muscle. Just adding weight in general will help me to be able to take on one of these guys." I nodded to the warriors on the other side of the room. They tended to keep to the male side of the room more than our side. That was strange considering they wanted to pick mates out of the women they abducted. "Why do you think they mostly stay on the other side with the guys?"

Betsy spoke up, "They probably have been warned to keep away from us for now. Look at what happened with Lisa last night. She's already been claimed, and she had only met the 3 aliens. My guess is that they are supposed to wait until all of them have had a chance to meet us then they can pick who they want and fight over us." She had this dreamy look in her eyes, like she was in some faraway place.

"Isn't it romantic to have an alien warrior fight over us? I wonder how many of them are on this ship? How big is this ship?" She let out a little giggle then covered her mouth so that no one could hear her.

Natalie looked at Betsy and squinted her eyes and shook her head. "What happened to you Betsy? Last night you were crying and trying to be as small as possible, and today you seem eager to mate with them. What's up with that?"

"Hey, I just happened to realize the situation. We are never getting home... I don't want to be a slave. Instead, I would rather have a warrior fighting for my love who will take good care of me." Betsy looked over to the three new guards we had today. None of them were looking our way. They had all picked out women in other cages to admire.

Lisa walked in at that moment with a tray full of what appeared to be our breakfast. It looked like we were going to get chalky jello mold again. I really hoped that wasn't on the menu for all of our meals this entire voyage.

She handed small trays of food to the girls in each cell as she made her way over to us. "Hey Lisa, how was it? Did he treat you nicely?" Natalie asked.

"Are you happy with your choice? And what's the rest of this ship like?" I asked as I reached out to take my plate, which again had a larger portion of protein on it.

"Rotna's a very nice man, or alien, whatever. Anyway, he kept his distance and let me get a good night sleep. This morning I was able to take a hot shower and eat food that is actually edible." She looked down at what she was handing us and made a face, like she was disgusted with what she gave us. "They have these machines that make food, kinda like in those sci-fi movies. And you can program different foods too. They even have Earth foods! I had bacon, eggs, hash browns, and coffee for breakfast. You all really should choose a mate as fast as you can." She moved to the next cell, the one she had been taken from, and spoke with her old cell mates.

I walked over to the other side of my cell, the side closest to her, "Lisa, how many aliens are on this ship? Did you get a good look?" I was holding onto two of the bars with my forehead leaning against the cold metal cell.

"I didn't see much, Rotna took me straight to his quarters where I fell asleep pretty quickly. This morning, he took me to their version of a mess hall where I got to eat anything I wanted. Then we went to another room where they were preparing your meals. Sorry this is all you get. I might be able to get them to let you guys eat something a bit better, in time." She shrugged her shoulders and turned back to her friends who also asked her how many aliens were on the ship.

"I didn't count, but I think there are more of them than there are of us. Trying to fight them won't work. The sooner you realize the situation you are in the better off you will be. Also, not all of the aliens are handsome. Some look more alien than others." She looked around at the women in the cells nearest her, and then her eyes roamed over toward the alien jailors who were watching her like a hawk.

"I better hurry up. I don't want Rotna to think I'm not

doing my part. But trust me when I say that so far you have seen the best looking male specimens on this ship. Don't take too long to grab one. Or you might be stuck with a real alien instead of a hybrid." She turned and walked to the other side of the room where the men were kept.

"What did she mean by hybrid?" I looked over to Natalie, and then back at Sheila, as my eyes widened. "Lisa, come back over here!" I yelled out to her. What she said about the aliens was sinking in, and my mind was going to strange places.

One of the warriors looked at me and said, "Be quiet and eat your breakfast."

I sat back down and ate what was on my plate, looking forward to the time when I would get to use the facilities. They took us in batches to use the restroom and clean up. Another group of aliens came in that we hadn't seen, and it appeared that Betsy might be right. They seemed to be taking turns monitoring us while checking us out.

Natalie looked up from her breakfast, "Sheila, do you see anyone here that tickles your fancy?" she looked at Sheila and smiled while raising her eyebrows up several times.

"Oh yes, there was one guy last night, and then two today. The one that really has me hot is the Commander. He's one sexy specimen! If Paris isn't going to take him, then I'm going to try claiming him as mine. Something tells me that he would take really good care of me." She started laughing and sat back down on the floor while checking out the remaining aliens in our jail.

"I can't believe you guys! How can you be thinking of hot aliens and how well they'll take care you? Why aren't we planning our escape instead?" I threw my hands up in frustration at them all.

Sheila scooted over and whispered in my ear, "They can hear us talking, so be careful what you say. But don't worry, we *are* going to get out of here." She winked at me, and I gave her a half smile.

That got me thinking, maybe I should play up the Commander angle. If he were to give me another chance, then I could use that to get more information and maybe find a way out of here, for all of us.

A few hours later the guards changed, and Venay came in with them.

He walked around and looked at everyone, including the men. Then he made his way to my cell last. "Paris, have you enjoyed the food and accommodations?" He gave me a small smile and put his hands behind his back.

"Honestly? I have not. Even though it is warmer and seems relatively safer than where I was, I think I still wish to go home." I stood up and walked over to where he stood and took in his appearance. He really was a good looking specimen of an alien. Could I do this? Could I really agree to mate with him in hopes of getting my freedom? But that would mean I would be agreeing to marry him. I always thought that I would be in love with the man I married and it would last forever, not just long enough for me to trick him and run away. *Desperate times call for desperate measures.*

"However, I am starting to realize that my life is no longer mine. Can I still take you up on your offer? I don't think I'm made for slavery." I reached out of the bars and touched his arm, then looked up at him through my eyelashes, "I know that I'm not going home now. Maybe I can make a life with you instead?" Then I slowly and lightly ran my hand down his arm while biting my lower lip.

He stood still and eyed me as he thought about it. His eyes moved up and down my body, or at least what there was of it. I knew I looked like I could use many hot meals, maybe this would get them for me. "Alright, I will give you a chance. But I don't want to hear any more about going home, and you are not to try and break free." He pointed a finger at me as he spoke.

"Where would I go now? I can't fly a spaceship, and we are already out of my solar system, aren't we? How would I get home?" I gave him a pout and tried to grab a hold of his hand but he moved it so he could open the cage. He put his hand up against a biometric lock that opened the door.

Venay looked behind me at the rest of the girls. "The rest of you stand back. Don't bother trying anything." He took a long look at someone over my shoulder so I looked back. It was Betsy he was staring at. She was looking down at the ground and shaking.

"Sheila, can you keep an eye on Betsy?" I looked from Sheila to Betsy, and that was when she noticed how frightened the girl was. She moved over to sit next to Betsy and put her arm around her.

"Sure thing. You go get cleaned up and put some meat on those skinny bones of yours, and I'll take care of Betsy." She gave me a smile as I walked out of the cell.

CHAPTER FIVE

"Venay, why do you allow young girls to be abducted? That girl Betsy, she's barely 18 and hasn't even finished high school yet." We were walking down the corridor to what I hoped was a real bathroom where I could take a shower, or better yet, a bath.

"She is of the correct age, our laws don't require that humans have finished school, just that they are at least 18. It wasn't always like that. But over the years the humans have worked with their mates to get us to see that we need to consider who we are taking. Young children for example, it would take years for us to raise them and then to consider what to do with them. Teenagers are nothing but problems. I guess those years of growing up and adjusting to your body's changes as either a human or a V'Zenian, are the same on both worlds." He put his arm around my shoulder, and guided me down another corridor until we stopped in front of a door.

I almost screwed my plan up. When he touched me my body wanted to tense up, but I had to remember that I needed to gain his trust in order to find a way off this ship.

In order to do that, I needed him to think I was falling for him.

There was another one of those biometric scanners next to it and he put his hand on it and the door swooshed open. "We agreed that the women, at least, needed to be grown up before we take them."

"She's way too young to be out here and having to deal with deciding to be a mate or a slave. You really should look for older women, not young adults." I peeked my head into the room I assumed was going to be my quarters for the duration of the journey. To my right was another room, the door was open, and it appeared to be a kitchen type of area. Against one wall in the room, a table and two chairs sat, as well as a short counter with two very different electronic contraptions on it. One looked like it might be some sort of futuristic microwave, but the other I had no clue. It was rectangular and metal with a lever on the right side. I couldn't tell how it opened.

Straight ahead was a sitting room. The chairs and sofa looked more comfortable than what was in that room where I first met Venay. Then to the left was another room, but the door was closed. The living room was furnished in muted tones of beige and silver. He really did need a woman's touch to make this a home and not just quarters on a ship. "How long do you live on this ship each year? Do you even have a home back on your planet?" I looked over to him and wondered what it would be like to be married to a man who spent most of his time flying the galaxy. I shuddered with the thought. But I wasn't sure if it was a pleasurable shudder or not.

"I spend most of the year traveling between our two planets, and only stay home for two months before I am off again. Our race is in dire need of an infusion of new DNA so I must find mates for as many males on my planet as I can. We also tend to go through a lot of slaves during the year it takes me to make a round trip." He sounded like it was no big deal to go through slaves by the dozen, it was as though he was talking about how often they needed new linen, not new human beings.

I eyed him warily. "Why do you need an infusion of new DNA?"

He looked at me with pursed lips. "We made some very large mistakes several centuries ago after a viral outbreak almost decimated my species. My ancestors locked themselves away and stopped intermingling with other families on my planet. This created an issue with mating; it started out as cousins mating with cousins, but as the blood lines were polluted, it became an even bigger issue than anyone realized." He stopped for a moment and took a heavy breath, then ran one hand down over his face before continuing. "Before anyone knew what was going on, most of the females on my planet were infertile. We already had an issue with low population, so the families started to merge again and tried to reverse the damage. With so few fertile females, we knew within a generation or two our species would die out." He shook his head as he looked across the room with a distant expression on his face.

I actually felt bad for his people. What would humans do if we were in a similar situation? We wouldn't give up and just die, that's for sure.

"We used to be a race ruled by royalty, similar to your kings and queens. But once we cut ourselves off from everyone, the lower class or servants became the only means to continue mating if we didn't want to mate with our brothers and sisters. After the royalty had all mated with their relatives, they decided to try mating with the servants only to find they had the same issue. No one thought anything about the servants or that they could have the same issues. So we merged the lower class with the upper class in a last ditch effort to keep our population alive. It may have given us one more generation." He took my hand in his and continued.

His hand was large in comparison to mine, but for some reason, it felt good. I shouldn't like this feeling. Hopefully, it's just because I felt bad for the plight of his people.

"We had space flight capabilities before the infection; we just stopped leaving the planet. It was thought that the virus which almost killed us all came from another planet. It was later that we realized it was a virus of our own doing. So the space ships were brought out, fixed, and we set out looking for a new species to keep our DNA going. We also needed more servants." He laughed at what he said.

"The first species we found that was bi-pedal, like us, were humans. But your kind was so backwards that we decided they were not advanced enough to help our DNA. We took those we wanted to be our slaves and came home with them. The journey was long and half of the warriors on the ship had taken human women as their mates before we returned. There were at least a dozen pregnant women who ended up giving birth to very healthy V'Zenian boys and girls. It was decided that we were to capture more women for mating and also to bring back the males of your species to be our slaves."

He let go of my hand and stood up and walked to the far wall where there was a small porthole, and he looked outside, "We were desperate to save our race. So we came back with multiple ships and picked up over one thousand humans."

I jumped up and gasped, "One thousand humans at one time? How did you do this, and why so many?" I looked at him with my mouth agape and narrowed my eyes. "How many of the women willingly mated with your kind on that trip?"

He lowered his head, "Not many, I am afraid. But after that we started to rethink our ways and each decade we see better and better treatment of the slaves. It has been over a century since it became law that the human women must choose to mate with us, we are not allowed to force ourselves on any woman. Nor would we want to. These are the women who are our mothers and sisters. We would not allow them to be treated so poorly, at least, not anymore." He looked at me and lowered his head in shame. I could see that he felt the guilt of what his ancestors did. Maybe he even felt guilty for his actions now.

"Venay, you are still abducting humans against their will and forcing them to serve you as slaves or be mates. Most of the women in your holding cells would never choose to be mated to your warriors if they met them back on Earth and were given a choice. Well, except maybe Sheila. But what you are doing is still wrong." I got up and paced the area in front of the sofa. My heart was breaking for all of the women and men who had been taken against their will and forced to do the unthinkable.

"Surely your population has grown, and you now have the ability to reproduce without the need of humans. How long have you been doing this?" I sighed and wondered what I would do if I were in his shoes and held the fate of my entire species in my hands. That couldn't feel good.

"It has been over two hundred years, and we still have not been able to instill enough of your DNA into our babies. While we have started to look more human, we still only have about a 50% reproductive rate. Even children born to a human and a V'Zenian might not be able to reproduce." He walked back to where I was standing and wrapped his arms around me.

I could feel his sadness, it was seeping into my bones. Something inside of me wanted to console him and tell him that everything would be alright. So I let him hold me while he thought about what his people had done, and what they were still doing to the human population.

"There are movements on my planet to stop the infusion of human DNA. But there isn't another option on the table. We have traveled to other planets and met other species, but none of them are as compatible with us as humans. Even more now that we have bred with your kind for so long. Most of my planet is now inhabited by VZ Hybrids."

It was at that point I interrupted, "What's a VZ Hybrid?"

"That is what I am, one parent is V'Zenian and another is human. Although, most who claim to be V'Zenian really have some human blood in them somewhere along the line." My stomach made a most embarrassingly loud sound at that point.

Venay pulled away from me and looked down towards my stomach. "I am sorry, I should have given you something to eat as soon as we arrived. I am sure what you have eaten so far hasn't been very filling or appetizing, has it?" He gave me a sad smile and walked toward the kitchen.

CHAPTER SIX

After a nice hot meal and a weird shower, alone thankfully, the Commander had to leave me. He was needed on the bridge, or whatever they called it. My only frame of reference for outer space and ships was all of the sci-fi shows I watched growing up. If Captain Kirk could see us now, I wonder what he would think?

I was forced to stay inside my new quarters the rest of the day. Venay had locked the door so I couldn't get out; I know because I actually did try. I ate a few things from the futuristic microwave, which turned out to be a food replicator. They had programmed some Earth items like cheeseburgers and pasta. At least I wasn't going to starve on this trip.

Venay came back hours later, and I was asleep on the couch. I didn't want him to think I was ready to share his bed, so I figured I would be sleeping on the couch for the foreseeable future. It wasn't too bad, and I slept quite well until he woke me up.

"Paris, what are you doing sleeping out here on the couch? You can sleep in the bedroom. That bed is quite comfortable." He sat down on the edge of the couch and rubbed my back as I tried to wake up. I had slept on my side since the couch wasn't very wide.

"This couch is comfortable; besides, the bed is yours. I know I agreed to be your mate, but I need to wait to get to know you better before I can marry you. Do you even have pastors on board to perform marriages?" I looked up to him wondering how it worked. Now that I had agreed to this I needed to know the details. Did they have the same anatomy as humans? I had to assume they did since they had been mating with us for almost two centuries now.

He smiled and leaned down to kiss my cheek, "You are so sweet. As Commander it is my duty to perform the cere-monies for any couples who wish to mate while on board my ship. My second in command will perform ours when the time comes." He ran his hand down my arm and held my hand in his. It felt warm and comfortable. It seemed strange that my small hand would fit in his giant one so perfectly. I caught myself and stopped that train of thought.

"Where is Lisa? Can I go see her or any other girl who has agreed to mate with your men?" I looked up at him question-ingly. This was the moment I was waiting for: would he grant me freedom while on his ship?

He eyed me for a moment and then responded, "For now I can't let you roam about freely. I will escort you or their mates will escort them here to visit with you. So far Lisa is the only one who has chosen a mate. I have heard that a few of the women have made some advances to my crew, but no one else has chosen as of yet." Venay got up and walked toward the kitchen. He looked over his shoulder and asked, "Have you had dinner yet?"

"No, I haven't, and I'm hungry. What's good?" I walked into the kitchen, and my stomach started to rumble. If I kept up this level of eating, I would put weight back on in no time. Part of me was excited for that prospect, but another part of me would be sad if I did find a way out of this mess.

"Venay?" I needed to talk to him, but I was hesitant. This was a sticky subject, and I wasn't sure what he was going to say, although, it would tell me a lot about his character. I took a seat at his small table.

"Yes Paris?" He put down our dinner plates, took a seat, and looked at me expectantly.

I scratched the back of my head and my right knee was bouncing so high it almost hit the underside of his table, "What are you going to do with the young girl who was in my cell?" I couldn't bring my eyes up to meet his, if his answer was not something I wanted, I knew I was going to either cry or get angry. Those two emotions would not help me in my situation.

He sighed, "Well, she is too young to allow anyone to choose her for a mate. Which only leaves slavery as an option for her. It isn't the best option, but my mother might need an extra hand. She has always treated her slaves with the utmost respect. I could reach out to her and request that she buy that girl, what was her name?"

I was so overjoyed that I jumped up and gave him a huge hug, "Thank you so much! It really means a lot to me that you would look out for Betsy. Will you tell your men that they are not to try and convince her to marry them or mate with them?" I sat in his lap and wrapped my arms around his neck and felt utter contentment for the first time since high school. My smile must have been quite large because he smiled back at me. It was the biggest smile I had seen on his face since meeting him.

"Yes, I have already told them to leave her alone. Several of us on this mission have decided that we will make sure the next batch doesn't include anyone under the age of 21. We all agreed that 18 was just too young for this life. Most of them made horrible mothers at such a young age or insisted on waiting to get pregnant. We even lost a few babies during birthing to very young mothers." While he was still smiling, I had stopped. I was happy that young girls wouldn't be taken again, but he still planned on taking women and men. The contentment I felt earlier was gone. In place of it was a hardening of my heart. This was a lesson for me, one I wouldn't soon forget.

I couldn't get comfortable with him. He'll take care of me as best he can, but he was still an alien who goes to Earth and abducts human beings to take back to his planet.

"Hey, what's the matter? I thought you would be happy with that?" He used one hand to move my hair away from my face.

I got up from his lap and went back to sit in my chair, "While I am grateful that you will take care of Betsy, I'm still disappointed that you'll continue to abduct innocent men and women from my planet. Isn't there something else you could do? Like maybe ask for volunteers or something?" I moved the food around on my plate with my fork as I had lost my appetite.

"I don't like this either, but it's this or let my species die out. We can't contact your Earthen Governments, they will not be able to handle this. Your species isn't ready for intergalactic relations with anyone, even if they are partly related now."

"I think letting us get used to this would be better than abduction and forced slavery. You don't seem to understand our past. Slavery is something that we dealt with a while ago. Our people are still very sensitive to this topic, as they should be."

"Yes, we know all about your history. We have even taken some of the humans who were slaves on your planet. Our history teaches that they were very happy to leave your world."

"Hmph, I doubt that very much. Being abducted from one bad situation, one where you understood the rules, and being taken to one where you don't understand? I think your history books were written to just make your kind look better." This discussion was not going well. I crossed my arms over my chest and stopped eating all together.

"I think I lost my appetite. What do I do with the left-overs?"

"Left-overs?"

"You know, the food I didn't finish." I still couldn't look at him.

"We don't need to worry about that. The food will get recycled and used again in the replicators." Venay didn't seem to have any issues with his appetite. He took several bites of his food as I spoke.

"Seriously? You can recycle the food and use it again? That is just the thing my people would love to learn about! I bet if you met with our leaders, they would be happy to exchange some of your technology for Earthlings who want to join you guys." The idea of hunger no longer being an issue sparked several ideas.

"As I said, you aren't ready. This topic is not one I wish to keep discussing. What do you want to do tonight?" The fierce look in his eyes told me to drop the topic, for now.

"Okay, fine, for now. Can I go see some of the women I know?" I eagerly asked.

"Yes, that might be a good idea. Show them you are happy with your choice and that you are safe as well."

We walked together to the room with the prisoners, as we walked I asked him more questions about the ship and how many were on it. Turned out he had another room of slaves.

Before we arrived to my old jail cell, I noticed a few of the crew members and how different they looked. "Venay, are all of the men on this ship from your planet? Or do you use crew members from other species?"

"They are all my species. As I said earlier, we have intro-duced human DNA into our society. Some believe that we should not have done that. They didn't like to mix species.

The results are what I look like. More and more of my species are turning out to look closer to humans than they do to the original V'Zenians. But this was expected. The small portion of those who claim to be pure bloods, are still trying to stick together, but are having trouble procreating. Somewhere along the line, I think some of them actually did mate with a human or two, their reproduction rates are slowly increasing."

"Wait, so there are some who still look like your kind did 200 years ago?" This was getting curious. I wondered if those were what I was seeing on this ship.

"Yes, I have a few purebloods on my ship. I doubt any of them will find a mate with your kind here, but they will have first pick of slaves when we get home. That is one of the perks of going on this long mission. You can choose your mate or slaves. They have to buy the slaves, but since they get the first pick, they get the better stock."

"Why do you do that? Call them stock? They're people, not cows." My blood pressure was rising. I could feel it. I could feel my face burning, and my fists were clenching. If I wasn't careful, I might chip a tooth from all of the grinding my teeth were doing lately.

"In our society, humans who aren't mates are no better than livestock. I have spent time on your planet learning about your societies. When slavery was legal on your planet, most slaves were no better than livestock to your ancestors," He countered.

"But we have evolved since then and know that slavery is wrong! All humans are to be treated as equals, no matter their race or background." Why couldn't he understand this? His mother was a human. What did she teach him?

He stopped walking, and I followed suit. "You would like to think you are better than us, wouldn't you? But you still have slavery, it might be illegal, but it still happens, and some governments turn a blind eye to it." He wasn't wrong.

"Yes, but there are a lot more governments working to stop it than not. We aren't perfect, far from it. But I do think we could help each other if we were to work together." I knew I wasn't supposed to mention that again, but I just couldn't help myself.

Venay had a scowl on his face, and started walking again, but said nothing. When we reached the door to my old prison, he stopped, "I have something I need to do so I will leave you here. You are free to roam the room, but you may not leave it unless a guard goes with you. I will return shortly."

He moved to put his hand on the biometric scanner, and I put my hand on his arm, "Thank you. I appreciate this chance to see the girls and to check on Betsy."

He grunted, nodded, and then the door opened.

As I walked into the room, everyone quieted and looked my way, "Hi everyone! I hope you're all ok?" Some greeted me with smiles and others with frowns. To be expected, they have been in this tight space for a while now with only that gross moldy thing they call food.

I walked over to my old cell and said hi to a few people along the way. Looking over toward the guys, I decided I would check on them too before I left for the night.

As I passed one cell, someone yelled out, "Traitor!" I didn't see who it was but I figured some would feel this way. I know I would if I were still in here without a way out.

I just sighed and kept moving until one woman asked, "How was it? Was he nice?"

"Um, he's ok so far. I'm sleeping on the couch until I'm ready to marry him. He isn't pushing the issue so far. And he said that eventually I'll be able to move around the ship by myself. So I guess that's nice?" I shrugged my shoulders and quickly walked over to Betsy.

"Hey there, how are you doing tonight? Any better than earlier?" I had worried about her all day.

"I'm okay, I remembered your Commander, he was there when I was abducted." Betsy looked down at her feet.

"Really? He told me he didn't like the idea of someone so young being brought on board." This was new information.

"I'm starting to remember a bit more, I'm not sure what they drugged me with, but I don't remember being abducted. I just remember seeing a couple of really good-looking men and then waking up here. But today, after he came to get you, memories started coming back. I think that's why I was afraid of him when he showed up."

I reached out to put a hand on her arm, "Hey, it's ok, he won't hurt you. I won't let him, or anyone else. He did agree that you shouldn't be coerced into mating with anyone since you are too young. So he is going to ask his mom, who is human, to buy you."

Her hopeful face turned to sadness.

"I'm sorry, I did try to get him to take you home, but he won't. His mom supposedly treats her helpers well. I think maybe we should think of this as an opportunity for you to become a helper. Maybe she will treat you that way too." I looked at her and then at the others in the cage.

"Betsy, do you have any experience cooking or cleaning?" I asked.

"I worked in a diner after school and on the weekends. I was a server. So I have that experience. Will that help me?" Betsy's face began to look hopeful again. I hoped she wouldn't be disappointed.

"Yes, I think it might. I don't know anything about them, but maybe we can get you an actual job as a waitress instead? I'm trying to talk to him about the possibility of abolishing slavery, but he isn't the one to make that call. Hopefully he can work to help make changes as time goes on. But, for now, let's just try to make things as good as possible for you." I smiled at her, and she gave me a shy, timid smile in return.

"I think I might like that better. I was trying to rally my

nerves and become a mate, but you're right, I'm not ready to be someone's wife or even a mother! But a server would be good, at least until you can get us home." Betsy's voice sounded stronger and I could tell we were headed in the right direction for her.

"Hey, now we talked about this today. I don't see how that is going to happen any time soon. Please don't count on that. It will only upset you even more." Sheila came over and was listening in on our conversation but then decided to join us.

"Sheila, do you really think we are stuck? That we can't get home?" I looked at her with pleading in my eyes. I didn't want to lose hope, and I certainly didn't want Betsy to either!

"Sadly, Paris, I do think we are stuck. It might happen down the road, but we are on a spaceship heading to a place we know nothing about. Even if we did find a way to take over the ship, how would we turn it around and go home? And don't get me started on the experiments our own government would do to us! Being in space, abducted by aliens? Come on, you know we wouldn't see outside for a very long time. If ever." Sheila arched a brow and pursed her lips.

She was right. I hadn't thought about that. Even if we did somehow force this ship back to Earth, our government would find out about us, and they would kidnap us and probably treat us just as badly, if not worse, than these aliens. Something else needed to happen before we could safely go home. I needed to get the V'Zenian government to make first contact with my own government. But that was a problem for another day.

Today, I needed to help my fellow abductees to find a better way to live. Sheila seemed like a leader, and she would help me, I knew it. But what could we do? Other than talk as many of the women as possible into marrying these aliens? And the men, well, I just hoped that they would be treated half-way decent. I thought that was the most I could hope for.

I spent the next hour chatting with the women in that area and then decided it was time to check on the men. One day soon, I needed to go into the other room with the rest of the abductees and check on them as well.

CHAPTER SEVEN

I hadn't met any of the men yet, so I was a bit hesitant to chat with them, but it needed to happen. Since the Commander had chosen me to be his wife, mate, whatever, I needed to use my position to do whatever I could to help them.

The way they looked at me was a surprise. Almost all of them had hostile expressions. Some were leering at me, some were scowling, and others wouldn't even look at me. The guards in the room noticed and two of them stepped closer to me. They gave the men dirty looks, I wasn't sure if they were trying to protect me. However, this was what I needed to do.

"Hi guys, I wanted to introduce myself and see if there was anything I could do for you?" My smile was a bit hesitant, but who could blame me with such animosity staring me down.

"Yeah, you can leave us alone, traitor!" A few of the men started calling me traitor, but for the most part, most kept quiet.

"Look, I know this sucks, but I'm trying to help you guys. I didn't ask for this, and I wasn't going to accept his offer when he first asked me, but after one day in here I knew what I had to do. If there is anything I can do to help, I will." I sighed and started to walk away when one guy stood up.

"Hey, you never did tell us your name." The man was tall, he was just over six feet by my guess. He had dark brown, wavy hair and hazel eyes. He could have been related to me, if all of my relatives weren't dead.

"I'm Paris, and you are?"

"A slave, from the looks of it." He laughed and looked at his fellow men, who started to laugh and joke with him.

"Well, if you want to be treated better, maybe you should think of yourselves as workers, instead of slaves. Slaves have no hope, and I intend on making sure you do have some hope. It may not be today, but down the road I *am* going to find a way to make things better for all of us."

"Don't include yourself in 'us,' sweetheart! You're not a slave or a worker. You gave in and agreed to be the Commander's whore! That's what any woman is who takes an alien mate!" He turned his back on me and slumped down to the ground with his friends.

I could tell this was going to be tough, and I intended to find a way to get them to trust me and for me to make life easier for them. But first, I needed Venay to trust me.

One of the guards came over, "Paris, don't mind them; they are just jealous they don't have the same options as the women. That is all it is. Trust me, they don't really think of you that way. He said that just to upset you and try to make himself feel better. All of the men do this every time. Why don't I take you back to your room? The Commander will join you shortly, I am sure." This guard was quite nice and walked me back to my new prison cell. Albeit, a much bigger and nicer cell, but a cell just the same.

"What's your name?" I looked the new alien up and down. He looked different than most of the other aliens I had met so far.

"Cazon."

"Cazon, you look a bit different than the Commander. Would you tell me about your parents? Are they both hybrids?" He had the multi-colored veins that were glowing, although not as bright as Venay's, but still stood out. The main difference was the color of his skin, it was more like an opalescent blue, but unlike anything I have seen on Earth. Well, maybe a custom paint job on a muscle car? As we walked along the corridor I could see the light hitting his skin, and it changed to different shades of blue. At one point, I thought I caught a purplish hue, but that couldn't be right. I wondered if it would it be rude to ask him.

He chuckled, "Humans are all alike, and you can't seem to stop categorizing each other by their skin tones. I find that strange. You have already abolished slavery, but you still segregate yourselves from each other, why is that?"

My eyes shot up, and I stopped abruptly, "You've already picked up on that? Wow, I'm impressed. You must have been paying very close attention to us or to our social media?"

"You might say that humans interest me. My parents are purebloods, but since not many of the pureblooded females give birth, I have been considering taking a human mate. That is why I am on this trip. I am lucky, I have three older siblings who have all taken pureblooded mates, so I am free to choose whomever I want. That is really the only segregation my species experiences. You are either pureblood or hybrid. But we are all V'Zenian." Cazon smiled but it didn't reach his eyes.

"Interesting, you do still segregate, just between two classifications. We may not be all that different after all." I furrowed my brow and considered how I could use this information to stop their abductions. Finding commonalities between our species might serve to make us look more even to them and in turn, could help to stop slavery of the human population.

"Maybe." He started walking again towards my cabin, and

I followed him. "But when we segregate, we don't hate like the humans do. Those of pureblood hope to keep our DNA intact, because if we don't, then we will eventually be more human and less V'Zenian. We will become a different species."

"I think there are those on Earth who feel the same way. They don't want to see races intermingling because then they become a different race, in their eyes. However, I have never seen it that way. In fact, my high school boyfriend was a different race than me, and no one ever looked down on us. I grew up in an area that had many races and many inter-racial couples. So, it wasn't as big of a deal for us." I tried keeping pace with the large alien, but his stride was much longer than mine. I ended up practically running to keep up with him.

"If you study the conflicts you will see more concentrations in different areas than in others. Places like Los Angeles, California have conflicts, but Orange County doesn't. Those two places are next door to each other. It is interesting, and something I always wanted to study. But, that is a very heated topic back home. I guess now the problem for us humans will be, human versus alien. I have a feeling that all of the different races you have on board here will eventually see all of us Earthlings as humans, and not see the different colors of our skin. What is it like with humans on your planet? Is there much racism there?" I was panting before long and needed to stop talking so I could catch my breath.

"You are correct in your assumptions, once the people on this ship integrate with the rest of the human population on my world, they will stop seeing color. You will see some hate towards those who mated with my species, but over time it dissipates and just turns to hate for their masters." Cazon must have noticed my heavy breathing because his steps slowed enough so I could walk at a brisk pace instead of almost a run.

"Hm, I see. Well, maybe if you guys would stop treating humans like cattle it would be different. Something to think about." Cazon had stopped in front of my door. His forehead was scrunched up tight and his lips were pursed.

I hoped he was seriously considering what I just said.

"Do you think that Sheila would consider mating with a pureblood? Or would she prefer a hybrid?" So that was what he was thinking about.

I laughed out loud as I realized he really wasn't paying much attention to our conversation and had drifted off into romance land.

"Well, she might if you romanced her and promised to treat her good. Are you considering mating with her?" I figured Sheila would most likely agree, as long as she found Cazon handsome.

He put his hand over the biometric scanner and my door opened, to an upset Commander standing there looking at me.

"Cazon, you may go. Thank you for bringing my mate back to me. Next time, make sure those human males don't treat her so poorly. Get her out of there before they can upset her or the other females in the room." He motioned for Cazon to leave. Cazon bowed and walked back down the hall before the door even had a chance to close.

"What were you doing talking to the male slaves? It's not safe until they accept their fate." He stalked over to me and suddenly stopped when he saw my face.

I could feel my face warming, and my eyes were narrowed on him. "I spoke to them because they are human! Maybe if you stopped treating everyone so badly they wouldn't act so awful. I actually think their behavior is spot on for their situation… Put yourself in their shoes." I put my hands on my hips and huffed out a deep breath.

"Paris, in my culture, I am actually treating them better than most would. They are slaves, that is all there is to it. If being my mate is going to be so difficult for you, maybe I should send you back to the cells?" He narrowed his eyes at me.

"Are you going to threaten me with slavery every time we have an argument? Cuz if you are, then we will not have a good marriage." Then I crossed my arms over my chest and thrust out my right hip.

"No, you are right. I shouldn't throw that in your face. I am sorry. This is all new to me. I never planned on finding a human mate, maybe not even mating at all. But when I saw you, I knew you were the one. This is an adjustment for me too. But I guess it isn't that big compared to what you are going through." He reached out to hug me, and I let him. Part of my brain was screaming at me to get the ugly, alien hands off me. But another part relaxed and enjoyed the comfort of a simple hug.

He wasn't trying anything untoward. His hands didn't roam anywhere, he just wrapped me in his warmth. Something I hadn't felt in a very long time.

"Yes, I guess it could be an adjustment for you as well. I'm not going to give up on better conditions for the, um, *slaves*," I stepped out from his embrace and looked down at my feet. "It is really important you understand that I will fight for freedom. You should expect that from most people on my planet, especially the Americans. We have a very strong sense of freedom and believe it to be our right, not a gift. We fight very hard to keep the freedoms that our forefathers died for."

"Yes, I have seen similar views by other Americans." Venay nodded. "Alright, how about I treat the, uh, *humans*, with as much respect as I can while they are on my ship? After that, I can't control what happens."

"Thank you, I would appreciate that. For starters, how about some better food? And is there anything you can do about their accommodations? Cells are not very comfortable."

Before he could answer me, he received a message from his second in command. The message comes from what appeared to be some type of hand-held communication device, like a walkie-talkie. "Sir, the human males have started to riot in their cells. The women are all very upset. I am not sure what happened, but Alpha Room is in absolute chaos. Should I knock them all out?"

"No, I will talk to them first. If that doesn't work, then we can use the sleeping gas. Send extra guards there too." Venay walked out of our cabin, and I followed him.

He stopped and turned around, "You can't go with me. They probably started the riot because of you. Please, go back into our cabin and wait for me." He reached out to open the door, but I stopped him.

"Venay, please. Let me speak with them. You and I were having a great conversation. Maybe if I tell them about what we discussed they will calm down and be better on the journey?" I gave him a tentative smile because I had no clue what he was going to do or say.

"Fine, but if I tell you to leave, you must listen to me and not argue."

"Deal!" I clapped my hands and was excited to try and find a way to help my fellow humans.

CHAPTER EIGHT

When we arrived at my old holding room, I knew it had to be those guys I was speaking to earlier. This was not the way to get what you wanted, at least not yet.

I followed Venay into the room; there were now over a dozen guards or warriors in the room. Some had different uniforms on. What looked to me to be warriors were the aliens with short swords on their backs and knives attached to a belt around their waist. These guys had much harder expressions and were even bigger than the aliens who had been guarding the humans up to this point. A few were even bigger and taller than Venay!

The regular guards had a police baton and what I thought was a Taser attached to their belts. But all of the guards had pulled out their batons for now. I just hoped they didn't have to Taser anyone before this was all said and done.

I stood to the left of the door and just watched what was happening with wide eyes. Venay probably wanted to address them before I said anything. And this was definitely more intense than I thought it would be.

"Give us our freedom!" shouted one guy. "Send us home!"

shouted others. "Let us go!" was being chanted by ten guys in another cell.

Venay walked over to the center of the men's area. "If you want to be treated better, you need to calm down and stop trying to cause a riot. You are here, and we are not going to take you back home. The sooner you accept your situation, the better for all of you!" He put one fisted-hand on his hip and the other he used to point at all of the men's cages.

One of the guys in the cell closest to him walked toward the bars and while holding them he said, "We don't want to be slaves. You abducted us, and we have the right to demand we go home now. You can't hold us against our will."

"You are quite wrong about that. I can do whatever I want with you. If you don't calm down I will have to sedate you. I really don't want to do that because it will cause the women to be sedated as well." Venay looked over towards the women and pointed, "See them, they look to be very frightened. Do you want to scare them? Or protect them?"

The same man said, "They have more chances of surviving this than we do. Why should I care about them? I heard what your guards were saying, most of them will choose to become whores to you alien scum! They are trai- tors! Traitors don't deserve to be treated well, they deserve death!"

A couple of the men nearby started chanting, "Death to traitors! Death to traitors!"

Venay looked back at me, "And you wanted me to treat them better? They would rather your women die than live as our wives, our mates. This is who you want to see get better treatment? This is who you want to set free on my home world?"

At that point, several of the men picked up what was left of their chalky jello mold and started to throw it at Venay and the other guards. Then a couple who were closer to the women threw some at them. The place was full of yelling and screaming. Some of the women cowered down in their cells and tried to get as far away from the men's cells as they could.

I walked towards Venay but was too close to one of the cells and a man grabbed my arm and pulled me closer to him. Just as I was about to kick at him, Venay jumped over and pulled the man into the bars and knocked him out cold. The guy released me as he fell down to the ground with a loud thud. Not one guy in his cell did anything to help him.

Several of the men who were chanting stopped and looked between Venay and me. Two of them pointed at me and yelled, "Traitor!" While another one yelled, "Whore!"

"Alright, that's it. Guards exit the room and release the gas." Venay looked at the men, "Just remember you brought this on yourselves. Paris was just now trying to negotiate better living conditions for you all while on this ship. You will not get anything extra from me anytime soon."

He walked over towards the women, "You might want to lay down now. You will be out cold the rest of the night, thanks to the men in this room."

Venay ushered me out of the room. I looked back at my new friends, eyes wide and wondered what would happen to them now.

Once we were all outside in the hall, a guard radioed in for something. Again I think he was speaking Klingon or some such nonsense. Then I heard the screams in the other room. Everyone was screaming for help. It sounded like some bodies thudded to the ground as well.

Down the hallway was an alcove that had a monitor which showed the holding cells. Venay showed me what was happening to the people in there. "Are you really just knocking them out? Or are they dead?"

"I should kill those men for what they did, especially the one who grabbed you! No one touches my mate!" He gently rubbed his hand on my arm, which looked as if it was going to have a bruise on it tomorrow. It was sore, but nothing compared to what everyone else was going through. I couldn't imagine how frightened they were. Did they believe it was just sleeping gas? Or did they think they were being murdered?

"Venay, they are very upset and jealous at the moment. I think in time they will see that the women are just doing what they need in order to survive. And if what you have told me about the mating bond is true, then some of the women won't even be able to fight off their attraction to your men or warriors, whatever. What do we call you anyway? Are you men? Warriors? What?"

He actually laughed, after all of that tension I was surprised to hear him laugh. "You can call us men. We refer to ourselves as males or warriors, depending on our ranks. Human interaction over the years has influenced us enough to use the term men, as well."

"What happens to that gas?" I pointed to the cloudy atmosphere shown on the monitors marked 'Alpha Room'.

"Once we are sure they are all asleep, we will reverse the airflow and all of that sleeping gas will be expelled into space. Then fresh oxygen will be pumped in. They usually sleep for a good six to eight hours."

"Ok, what happens tomorrow?"

"That depends on them. If they are calm, then they will continue to be fed. If they are still calm the next day, we will start the universal translator implantations. We will start with the females. The males usually accept it better after seeing the women go through it with no adverse side effects." He put his arm around me and guided me toward our quarters.

"Is it safe? Will the alien technology be accepted in our bodies?" I chewed my lower lip, worried about the idea of an alien doctor implanting something into my body. I knew the sci-fi shows were make-believe, but still, the idea of alien electronics inside of me frightened me. My mind was telling me that they were up to no good and the device might do something evil, like control me. I was not going to become a robot to alien masters.

"They are the same devices that we have implanted in us. There is also a communication node that some will have installed and some won't. I would hope you would agree to have it installed so that you and I may communicate directly. It is also helpful should you ever get lost on our planet, as you can just call me and as long as there is an open line, I can get a general idea of where you are. The GPS isn't exact in these things, and it would never give away your identity."

"Sooo, if you wanted to track me you could?" I bristled at the thought of having a lo-jack installed in my brain.

"No," Venay chuckled. "The line of communication between us must be opened. In order for me to get a general fix on you. If I went looking for you, I would not be able to find you. It works similar to your cellular phone technology. I can't find you unless we are communicating. However, I can see if any of my warriors are in a certain area. We all have them installed in case of crashes. While we won't know who is where, we can tell if there is a warrior in a general area, just not who it is."

"Um, ok. I'll think about it. That might be helpful, if you promise me it isn't a tracking device." I believed him, but was still a bit leery of anything he had to say. If I was going to try and get away, I couldn't very well do that if he could track my location at any time.

CHAPTER NINE

Early the next morning, Venay came out to the living room and woke me up. "You know, you don't have to sleep out here. I promise nothing will happen until you are ready. This couch isn't very comfortable for sleeping."

Rubbing the sleep from my eyes, I turned over on my back. "It's much better than what I've had for the past five years. I don't think I've slept that good since I moved to the streets." I smiled and started to get up from the sofa, but Venay put his hand on my shoulder.

"What do you mean? Have you not had a home to sleep in these past five years?" His brow furrowed and a storm appeared to be brewing behind his eyes.

I could see the pity coming. It was always this way. Whenever someone found out I was homeless they would look at me with pity in their eyes, their eyebrows would pull down in concentration, and they would give me long hugs or rub my arm.

I didn't want anyone's pity or sadness. These things happen. But I wasn't going to rehash the events with him, not yet anyways, "Yes, I was homeless, but let's save that story for another day. I really want to see how everyone is doing after last night. Can we go to the holding cells after breakfast?"

"I think that can be arranged. I was heading there first thing myself, but the same rules apply, plus one. I don't want you anywhere near the men for now." He arched an eyebrow.

I pursed my lips and sat up on the sofa. "But why? I need to try and gain their trust, and talking to them will help. I promise I won't get too close to the cells again. How about that?"

"No, I don't want you anywhere near them, for now. Once I believe they will treat you with more respect, I will allow it. But until that day, I don't want you anywhere near them. Do you understand? This is for your own protection, please don't fight me on this." He sighed and looked down at his hands.

"I don't think I could stand it if they hurt you. If something happened, my anger would get the better of me and they would not survive the trip home." He looked up at me with sadness on his face, and he reached over to me and brushed the hair out of my eyes.

I really needed to get a haircut. But that wasn't something one spends money on when they were homeless and jobless. What money I did receive, went to food for Lola and myself. Once in a great while, I would treat myself to a Peppermint Mocha from my favorite coffee house, but I guess those days were over.

"Ok, I can understand. But please know that I can take care of myself. I survived five years living on the streets and not once did I lose a fight. You'd be smart to realize I'm not soft. I may not look like much, but I'm pretty scrappy when I need to be." I reached out and squeezed his hand as I stood up.

After a wonderful breakfast of pancakes and bacon, we made our way to the holding cells.

They had just received their morning meal, although I

don't think it could really be called a meal. Just thinking about how that chalky jello felt going down my throat was making me gag. It was like someone took a jello mold and covered it with a white, powdery residue that was thick and stuck as it made its way down my esophagus. I knew I made the right choice in agreeing to be Venay's wife. If for nothing else, real food.

He greeted the guards, which had tripled since last night. Then we walked over toward my old cell mates. "Sheila, Betsy, how are you two doing? What happened when you woke up?"

They were sitting on the ground, leaning against the bars. Neither looked very good. Most of the women had a greenish tint to their skin and bags under their eyes. They were all sick.

"Not good. Those stupid men are going to get us all killed. I swear, the first guard who wants me, can have me. I'm not going through this again." Sheila didn't move, but she did turn her eyes towards me for a second.

I had put a couple of pieces of bacon in my pocket. Carefully, so Venay didn't notice, I pulled them out and gave them to Sheila and Betsy. Then I whispered, "I'll try to bring you more real food later."

Venay was looking at me closely, so I got up and moved over to the next cell. "Natalie, are you ok?" She looked sick, but much better than Sheila or Betsy.

"I'm ok. I hope those idiot animals who call themselves men learn to calm down. I don't think most of us could take another night like that." She had this far off look on her face, like she couldn't focus her eyes or something.

"I'm so sorry you had to go through that. I'll see what I can do to help you guys." I reached in and squeezed her hand and then walked over to Venay.

"Commander, would it be alright if I addressed the men in here? I promise I won't get close to them, I just want them to understand a few things." Doing my best to keep a calm face, I waited patiently for his response.

He scratched his chin, "Ok, but if it gets bad, then you are not coming back here for a few days. Understood? I can't have them causing problems again so soon."

"Understood, and thank you." I smiled at him and walked a bit closer to the men's side.

I raised my eyebrows and took a few tentative steps away from the men and closer to Venay. "Ok, well, gentlemen, I have been trying to broker a deal for you. One where you will be treated more humanely and at the very least get better food. In fact, you would have had a decent meal today if you hadn't tried to start a riot and scare the pants off the girls over there." I pointed to the women's side of the room.

"I doubt very much that the Commander will allow you anything other than that gross pasty stuff they call food, at least for a while. But if you will agree to act like men, and not animals, I will see what I can do for you." I turned my back to the men and faced Venay.

"Commander, since the women have been scared to death, and remained quiet, may they have comfort food for lunch today? I saw your replicators have macaroni and cheese. Would that be alright for them?" I looked pleadingly into his eyes.

He huffed and looked over to the women, "Yes, I suppose that would be fine. But we need to add some protein to the meal. They are going to need it after last night."

"Thank you, I'm sure they'll enjoy chicken with their meal too. May Lisa and I start making this up for everyone?" I needed all of the prisoners to see that I was subject to Venay, but that I was also trying to work for their betterment as well. It was the only way I could envision getting their trust. I wasn't just going to roll over for the alien, I was going to use my position to help my own people.

The men on the other hand, well, that would be a

different fight. I should have known they wouldn't have been good for much longer. None of them appeared to be fighters, however a couple did look like they could be leaders. I only hoped they didn't lead the men into death.

I just needed to get them to work with me.

"Yes. Cazon, please escort Paris to find Lisa and start making the noon meal for the women. The men will continue to get what they have been getting so far." He looked over at the men and then at the women.

"How about the men in the other holding room, how have they acted?" Venay asked.

"Sir, they have all been relatively calm. So far, they haven't said much other than ask what is going on." Cazon responded.

"Okay, beta room can have what Paris suggested as well, including the men. But I want to know if they act up at all." Venay turned and headed out of the room. When he passed me, he quickly grabbed my hand and lightly squeezed it before leaving.

I followed Cazon out of the room without giving the men a second look.

"Hey, does that normally happen on these journeys?" I asked once the door had closed.

"This is only my second one, but from what I hear, it happens almost all of the time. There is always a troublemaker." He eyed me up and down. "But you are different. I have seen women try to persuade the Commander to do a lot, but he has never given in. You must be his true mate for him to soften towards the slaves."

"Trust me, he isn't soft." I huffed and it was almost a snort, as I thought back to what I had to agree to in order to get this. Going forward, I was going to have to be very careful with what I said to Venay, or he could take away the regular food and put them all back on chalky jello. I shivered thinking about that.

When I found Lisa, she was in her cabin reading. Apparently, they kept a nice collection of Earth books. Something to remember to check out later. "Lisa, can you help me prepare Mac 'n' cheese with chicken for the women? Even the men in the second room get it for dinner as well." Then I whispered, "Did you hear about the men trying to start a riot?"

"Yes, I did. How did it end? Did they get gassed?" Lisa put the book on the table next to her.

"Yes, the entire cell block did. Everyone is pretty sick too. I got Venay to agree to feeding everyone but the trouble-makers better food. The guys in our old cell block have to eat that chalky stuff for all of their meals until Venay changes his mind. I hope they settle down. Do you think they will? What have they said to you?" I sighed and realized I had a long road ahead of me with the stupid men.

I was all for fighting, but only when it made sense to do so. We would have to work together and find a way to break everyone out of the cells and then find a way to take over the ship. I doubted any of the humans could fly it back to Earth. We were going to have to find some aliens who sympathized with us.

"Come on, follow me to the mess hall where we can start preparing lunch for them. The replicators there are much bigger and can accommodate all of the, uh, guests? Geesh, what should we call them? I just can't think of them as slaves or even as prisoners! This really sucks." She motioned for me to follow.

"So far, it's just you and me. I know a couple of the women have made some advances on the guards, but none have accepted yet." Lisa's face screwed up and I followed her out of her quarters.

As we walked to the mess hall, we chatted about some of the potential couples. "Do you think Sheila will have someone within the week?" I asked, really wanting to know if we could recruit her out to help us.

"I'll be surprised if she doesn't snag a guy in the next two days! That woman is like a cougar." Lisa giggled. "Did you see the young guard she was eyeing right before the Commander came for you? He couldn't have been more than 21, and she's what, 35 or older?" Lisa asked.

We both laughed, and I realized that this was the first time I felt like I was going to be okay on this journey. Shoot, it was probably the first time I felt okay in a very long time.

We filled up two carts and took them to the other cell block. Lisa informed me that room was called the Beta Room. Our old room was the Alpha Room. Really imaginative names. But that's aliens for you.

The men in there did seem a bit more docile, from a distance. We gave the women their lunches first, and then Lisa and I both pushed our carts to the men's side, with Cazon trailing us the entire way. The way he was acting, it felt like he was my own personal bodyguard. He followed Lisa to the cell on the other side of the room and was talking to a guard there.

I stopped at the first cell and handed the guys their meal trays. One guy asked, "Is this for real? Are they giving us mac 'n' cheese today?" His eyes were wide, but his mouth was squished in disgust.

"Yes, I had to work with the Commander to get you this stuff, instead of the chalky jello stuff you've been eating. What's wrong, you don't like pasta?" I couldn't imagine them complaining about getting real food. What was up with them?

"This stuff is for kids, not adults," He huffed.

"Well, if you don't like it, I'm sure someone else will eat it for you. But this is what you're getting today." I bristled at his ingratitude.

"And what are you getting?" He leered at me, and I felt disgusting with the way his eyes looked me over.

"None of your business. Now eat your lunch and shut up." The sooner I got out of there, the better.

He dropped his meal tray and reached outside of the bars to grab my arm, "Oh, I think I know what I'm having, and you are going to be my ticket out of here. You're her, aren't you? The Commander's mate, or whatever you're calling yourself?" He was holding my arm very tightly, and it hurt. This was the other arm, now I was going to have matching bruises. Venay was going to be livid.

I looked at him with so much anger, I was surprised he didn't burst into flames, "Let.Go.Of.Me.Now!" I growled at him.

He tried to pull me closer to him, but I pulled back.

"Or what, you'll make me your personal slave?" He tried laughing, at least until I punched him in the throat. Then he let go of me and started coughing.

One of the guys in his cell said, "Serves you right, man. She's one of us. So what if she is doing something to make her life better. At least she brought us something besides chalk for lunch."

Another guy said, "Don't bite the hand that feeds you man." And then they laughed at the guy on the floor.

"Hey, don't mind him. He's been in a foul mood since we all woke up in here. There's nothing we can do until we land this stupid ship, right? So why make trouble now?" He shrugged his shoulders and took his meal to the other side of the cage.

He seemed to be a bit smarter. Fighting now would do no good. I hoped they would hold out until we landed.

Cazon made his way back to me and asked what happened. When I told him, he took out his Taser gun and shot the guy. Everyone who was near him, backed away quickly with their arms up. The guy I was talking to just a minute before said, "Hey now, we weren't involved. I even told him he was stupid to do that."

"Understand this, any man who lays a hand on the Commander's mate will suffer the same, or worse! Now shut up and eat your lunch. You have Paris to thank for the change in menu. But don't expect this again for a while. The Commander is going to be very upset about this." Cazon put the taser back on his belt.

Cazon walked me to the next cell and every man after that looked at his plate and thanked me. None of them would look me in the eyes.

Once we were out of that room, Cazon said, "For the next room, let Lisa feed the men. You stick to the women. I don't want the Commander to take his anger out on me or any of the other guards if you get hurt."

He looked at my arm, "Ouch, that looks like it will bruise. He is going to be very angry. Maybe I should just take you back to your room?"

"No, I'll be fine. One stupid guy isn't going to ruin my day. Besides, I want to see some of the women I've met so far. And you know, Sheila is in the other room, maybe we can spend some time chatting with her?" I raised my eyebrows up and down suggestively at him and giggled.

After Cazon walked in front of us, Lisa asked, "What's that about?"

"I think he might like Sheila. He was asking me about her yesterday." She gave me a knowing look, one more woman to add to our little group of couples. This was going to be fun … I hoped.

CHAPTER TEN

Handing out lunches in the next room went much better than I thought it would. Lisa handled the men, who pretty much ignored her. Then she came over to help me pass out the nicer lunches to the women who all really appreciated it.

"Sheila, what do you think of Cazon?" I asked as I handed her the lunch tray.

"He's pretty cute, but he doesn't pay me much attention. He seems to follow you around a lot." She narrowed her eyes at me.

"Yes, well, the Commander kinda got on him yesterday for allowing the men to talk to me so rudely. So, he's taking the protection part a bit seriously." I shrugged. "I barely made it in this room today. We were just next door with the other group of men," I looked down at my feet, this was awkward. "They were rude to me as well, and one of them grabbed my other arm, it's going to leave another bruise. Venay's going to be really upset when he sees it. Anyway, I gave the guy what he deserved, but Cazon tasered him! It was pretty crazy." I couldn't help the chuckle that came out. Now that I was away from the guy, it did seem a bit wild.

"Seriously? That's hot! Hmmm, I might have to try and

get his attention when he comes back, without you." She looked him over like a piece of meat in the grocery store. I swear she's a man-eater. Something told me that no human man would be able to handle her, only an alien. I chuckled as I thought about poor Cazon. Sheila was going to eat him alive.

"Please do, Sheila. I hope you're mated to him soon. It'll be much more fun to have you outside the cages with Lisa and me for the rest of this trip." I looked over to Natalie and wondered what she was going to do. One of the guys wanted her, but she didn't seem ready to give up on her fiancé yet. I couldn't blame her though.

Cazon came over to us and smiled at Sheila, "Hi there, Sheila, is that pasta dish really something human women like?" He pointed his head toward the dish in her hands.

"Sure is, we call this comfort food. Always reminds me of when I was a kid and mom would make me mac 'n' cheese on rainy days. She would cut up hot dogs and put them in too. Time was so much simpler back then." She sighed as she looked off into space remembering her childhood.

"Thank you for allowing this. All of us appreciate it, a lot." Sheila smiled coyly at Cazon and tilted her head a bit to the side. He walked closer to her, and I took that as my cue to hand out the rest of the lunches.

They chatted for a while. Once Lisa and I were all done, we went over and spoke with Natalie.

"Hey, do you think we can put in order requests?" Natalie asked.

I nodded as I thought about it. "I don't see why not. What do you want for dinner?"

"Could we have cheeseburgers and fries? I haven't been allowed to have that for months. My fiancé said I needed to lose some weight before we got married. Guess I had gained a few pounds since college. He wanted the girl he met in college not an overweight, old lady." She sighed and looked down at her skinny thighs.

"Um, Natalie, did he always say rude things like that to you? Cuz you are super skinny. Do you even have any meat on your bones?" I hated men who said things like that to their girlfriends. They had some issue with themselves, so they wanted to make everyone around them feel bad as well. Not cool!

"Only since I put on a couple of pounds. I was about five pounds lighter in college. It was probably because I walked a lot back then. Now I work in an office and sit all day. Well, I did, before this happened." She looked around the room and spread her hands out to gesture where she was.

"What a tool!" Lisa blurted out. "No man should say stupid stuff like that to a woman. You are better off without him."

"Hey, he loved me, and was always buying me presents. I didn't hear much praise from him, but he was going to make a wonderful husband. He had it all planned out. We were getting married this summer, and then I would keep working for two years. After that I would get pregnant and quit my job when the baby was due. I would stay home and take care of the house and kids. We wanted four kids. Ben, that's my fiancé, had a great job with a bank. He traveled more than I liked, but he would have provided for us so well." She hung her head and a silent tear escaped her eye.

"Ok, we need to change the subject here. Cheeseburgers and fries for all tonight!" I cheered and threw up one hand for a high five with Lisa.

"Sorry to break it to you, but the men don't get anything but the standard fare tonight. I doubt the Commander will ever give them anything else, not after last night." Cazon had come over to escort us out.

He put his hands on our back and ushered us out of the

room. I looked back over my shoulder, "Natalie, all of the women will have cheeseburgers and fries tonight, I promise!"

After we left the room and turned the corner to head back toward Lisa's room, I asked, "Cazon, you gonna take Sheila out on date and woo her? I think she'd love a date with you. Don't you Lisa?"

"Oh yeah, she would say yes in a heartbeat!" Lisa giggled.

He laughed and said, "Yeah, yeah, make fun of me. I doubt she will be easy to convince that I am her mate." He sighed loudly.

"Wait, you think she's your real mate?" I asked.

"Yes, I felt the pull towards her. She is the one for me. I wish it was the same for humans, it would be so much easier." He ran a hand through his hair, a gesture which made me think he might be nervous.

"Cazon, just ask her. I have a feeling she might be feeling that mating bond as well. She likes you. Just talk to her about it." I smiled at him and hoped he would man up … or warrior up? Whatever they called themselves he needed to step up.

"Yeah, maybe I should. That way I would know for sure if she is interested or not." He nodded while looking ahead.

"Why are you so nervous? You're a big, handsome warrior. You should be very confident in yourself." Lisa joined in on trying to encourage him.

"Most human women don't like to mate with purebreds on my planet. So we usually have a hard time convincing them. Most of the purebreds who have wanted a female had to buy her, and then wait for her to fall in love with him. It isn't a very good way to start off a relationship, but that is how most of us do it." He stopped in front of Lisa's door.

I asked, "Do you mind if I hang out with Lisa for the afternoon? She has some books and I would love to read them. Since Venay is working, it's probably best Lisa and I stay together anyway."

He shrugged, "I don't see why not. Use the communicator on the wall to call for me or the Commander if you want to go back to your room before anyone comes for you. I have to get back to the holding cells." He walked away after opening the door for us.

Once we were inside, we went and sat on Lisa's couch. "Ok, so what are you thinking? Do you want to go through with your mating ritual with Rotna? Or do you want to find a way home?"

"Would you be upset if I said mating ritual?" She bit her lower lip and rubbed the back of her neck while watching me for my reaction.

"I wouldn't be upset at all. You feel the call towards him, don't you?" I sighed and wasn't surprised.

"Yes, I do. My life back on Earth was fine, but this seems so much more exciting. Don't you think?" Lisa's eyes widened and her smile covered her entire face, it was so huge.

"Well, I haven't slept or eaten this good in years. I could get used to this, although I'm going to wait and see what happens when we get to their home planet. For all we know, we could be their food source! You know, like that movie, *Soylent Green*?" I shivered thinking about how that movie used people as their food source and most didn't even know it.

"Oh gross! I never saw that movie. Really? Cannibalism?" Her nose scrunched.

"Well, they didn't really know it. People would die early, you could only live so long in that dystopian society, and then they would be taken to a processing center where they would be turned into food bars. No one really knew that it was happening, well until the main character figured it out and tried to expose them. It is really a great show about corporate greed and government corruption. But also gross." I had to laugh in order to get rid of the heebie jeebies I was feeling at that point. My skin was crawling with what felt like a thousand ants.

Lisa didn't seem to like it either, "You don't think they are using us as food do you?"

"No, I don't. I just have an overactive imagination and a penchant for old TV shows and movies. Sorry if I scared you. Have you ever watched *Star Trek*? The ones from the eighties?" I asked Lisa.

"Um, no. That was before my time. I have watched the new movies and really like Bones, the doctor. He's hot!" She laughed and I joined her.

"Did you ever hear of a character named, 'Worf'? Cuz Venay reminds me of him." I chuckled a bit as I was mentally comparing Venay to Worf.

"Really? You think Venay might be a character from a TV show?" She sat back and eyed me like I was crazy.

"I have a *Star Trek* fetish, so sue me. I always loved Worf. He's one of my favorite characters from all versions of *Star Trek*, TV and movie. He had a great sense of honor and duty and always tried to do the right thing. Just like Venay. Oh wow, is that why I'm into Venay?" I looked up at Lisa and narrowed my eyes and chewed on my lower lip while thinking about the similarities between the two men.

Does he remind me of Worf? They're both very tall, handsome males. Both are part human and part alien, and so huge! When I was younger I used to fantasize what it might be like to date Worf, he was my TV boyfriend for a long time…

Lisa laughed, "You really do have issues you know? Thinking your alien commander is the same as a movie character! You crack me up. But seriously, are you attracted to Venay? Do you feel the mating bond?"

"I'm very attracted to him, but those similarities are probably why I feel so strongly about him. All through high school I watched the old reruns of *The Next Generation* and fell in love with Worf." I scratched my head. "Huh, that makes more sense than this mating bond thing. I bet I'm into Venay because he's so much like the character of Worf, besides the obvious physical differences. Inside, where it counts, they seem to be very similar."

I couldn't believe I was beginning to trust Venay and felt he had honor. What was wrong with me?

"Ok, whatever. You like the Commander, so what are you going to do about it?" She leaned forward and put her hands in her lap.

"Do? Nothing, for now. I need to get to know him better and try to figure out how we can help get the humans better treatment." My people were so much more important than my crush on an alien Commander.

"Sorry, I hate to break it to you, but there's nothing you can do about them. The Commander can control the treatment of our people here, on his ship. But once we get to their planet? I think it will take a lot longer to get something done. So, you better hurry up and marry that guy and get him on your side." It was sad to think that Lisa was already believing their story.

"Really, you don't think I can change the minds of all of the aliens on this ship? Get them to stop thinking of humans as their slaves? The idea has to start somewhere, doesn't it?" I got up and started to pace the room.

"Well, that might help. But none of these warriors have enough political clout to do anything. They might be able to help you get in touch with those who do. So maybe if you make friends with the right V'Zenians? I'm not really a political person so I can't help you here." She shrugged her shoulders as though it was no big deal.

Maybe I was taking this too seriously? Or was I just naïve enough to think that I could really do something about this? I wasn't really sure.

Cazon interrupted us at that point by ringing the bell.

Lisa invited him inside, "Paris, the Commander would like to meet you in your quarters. I am to escort you back now. Later, someone else will come by to get you so you can help feed the, um," He scratched the top of his head. "Humans? Yes, you can help feed the humans later on tonight." He smiled and motioned for me to follow him. It seemed like he was trying to stop referring to them as slaves, so that was a start.

We were both in our own little worlds as we walked back to my quarters. It was a nice, companionable silence.

Cazon opened my door for me, and he walked away as he said goodbye. I walked into my quarters and stopped, I couldn't believe my ears or my nose. I smelled something heavenly coming from the kitchen, and I could hear romantic music playing from somewhere in the room.

I turned to my right and headed towards the kitchen where I could hear Venay moving around and making some racket, with what sounded like plates and silverware. It was a bit early for dinner, but maybe his schedule today didn't allow a regular dinner time?

"What's this?" I looked around with wide eyes taking in the very romantic scene. "Is that Barry White I hear playing?"

"Yes, do you like it?" Venay had this silly grin on his face.

"I do. It's very romantic. How… who helped you to set this up?" My cheeks were burning and I hoped my face wasn't red.

"I did it all myself. The Commander of this cruiser doesn't really have anyone to go to when trying to learn how to romance a human female. We have some files on Earth cultures and some videos, and this is what I found that was the most often used song and type of dinner when a man loves a woman." The crooked smile on his face warmed my heart.

I went over to him, hugged him, and then kissed his cheek.

"This is very sweet and romantic, thank you. What prompted you to do this?" I took two steps back from his warmth.

"I heard what you said to Cazon the other day, and I decided to romance you and see if I could get you to fall in love with me. Earth customs are so foreign and strange to us. In V'Zenian culture, when you meet your fated mate, you both just know, and there is no need to court or romance the female. You both talk about it, and then decide to mate. We do have a mating ceremony, but it is more a formality. We never divorce or split up. We don't cheat on each other. Life is much simpler when we are with the one who we are fated to spend the rest of our lives with." He pulled back a chair and motioned for me to sit.

He was being a perfect gentleman. The table was covered with a red cloth, and there were two pillar candles sitting on it burning. I couldn't help but smile. I had never been on a date like this. The last time I dated was in high school, senior prom. We went to an Applebee's with a group of friends and then on to the dance. It was not romantic, but it was fun. The last time I had fun in fact.

"Yes, that does sound so much easier. I wish it was that way for us too. Some believe in soul mates, but even those will sometimes divorce. People fall in and out of love all of the time on Earth. I wish we didn't, but we do." I shrugged my shoulders. There was nothing I could do about the millions of people who divorced all of the time. It would be nice to have a fated mate, and never have to worry about divorce or cheating. I think our society would be much better off for it too.

"We experience love right away once we meet our mate. Don't you feel it with me?" He took my hand in his after he sat down across from me at the dinner table.

"You're in love with me? Already?" I could feel me eyes widening and was surprised at his confession. "But we just met a few days ago. How could that be?" I had never believed in love at first sight.

He chuckled, "Yes, I am already in love with you. You may not feel the mating bond, but I do. That bond is what helps me to love you. I hope in time you will love me in return." He leaned down and kissed my hand. The warmth of his lips sent shivers down my spine.

"Um, I mean, wow. That, well it sounds really nice, but dinner is getting cold." I felt my cheeks heat with either embarrassment or excitement. I couldn't be sure since this was the first time I was out with a man, even if he was an alien. "And yes, I hope to be able to return your feelings as well. For us humans, instalove isn't something we feel very often. So, it might take some time."

What was I saying? What was I feeling? Instalove? Stink! I might actually know something about that after all. If I fall in love with this guy, alien, whatever, then I am never getting home and neither are any of the people on this ship. I needed to keep a clear head here.

He served me a wonderful dinner of roasted chicken with rosemary potatoes, steamed green beans, and a red wine I had never heard of. "Did you get this wine from Earth? Or is it something the replicator made for you?"

"I picked up all of this food on Earth. Whenever we stop off we also fill up on basics like real meat, potatoes, and a few cases of wine. Earth wine is very popular back home, and we can sell it for quite a profit." He cut into his chicken and took a bite.

"So, you can cook real food? Not just replicate?" A warning hit me, and I was worried. Maybe Venay would romance me into liking him. Keeping a clear head was going to be very difficult if he kept this up.

He laughed a hearty laugh, "No, the food goes into the replicator storage system, and then we can make Earth meals very easily. Once the fresh food is gone, our replicator uses the basic proteins and nutrients we store on board to make our food. But for some reason, your food just tastes better when we use fresh ingredients from your planet." He smiled and squeezed my hand.

For some reason, every time he did that, I felt at peace. Like I was loved and protected. I guess I was if I really thought about it. He had already confessed his love for me and shown me he could and would protect me.

Once dinner was over, we moved into the living room and Venay asked me, "Would you like to dance?"

Oh boy! I wasn't sure what to do. Other than the prom and a couple of high school dances, I didn't dance. "I would love to, but I don't really dance. Do you know any Earth dances?"

"Yes, I have been to some nightclubs on Earth and took some lessons a couple of times. I really like one of your TV dance shows. Ballroom dancing can be fun. Do you know how?" He took me in his arms and we started to move to the music. We were moving quite well as long as I didn't think about it. As soon as I started to think about the steps I would mess up. Venay knew how to lead. A true alpha, so far, in every sense of the word.

When the music changed to another soft and slow song, he changed it up so that we weren't really dancing, it was more like swaying to the music. Venay used this opportunity to wrap his hands around my waist and pull me up close against him. I put both of my hands around his neck. He was so tall I could barely get my arms around him, but it felt like I fit perfectly. My head rested on his chest … and it felt like heaven. His heart beat was steady and strong under my head.

We continued to sway to the music for a couple of songs, not talking, just moving together as one. I closed my eyes and was surprised to feel I felt safe in his arms. A voice in the back of my head was trying to tell me something, but I ignored it. It felt too good to worry about anything.

He leaned down and whispered in my ear, "Are you enjoying this night?"

I whispered against his chest, "Yes, very much." I sighed contentedly.

He lightly kissed my ear, and I felt shivers go down my back. We hadn't kissed yet. Would this be the night we kissed for the first time? And I don't mean the sweet kisses on the cheek kinda kiss, but the kind that would tell me if he was the man for me or not. Did I want him to kiss me? The night was perfect. I didn't want to ruin it by pushing away from him. However, was I ready for this?

His lips kept brushing lightly along my jaw, stopping every couple of seconds to kiss me. Then when I thought I was going to die from the wait, his lips met mine. It was soft and sweet at first, but as soon as I kissed him back, he put more pressure on my lips, and then lightly nipped at my lower lip. This caused me to moan and I opened my mouth when his tongue stroked my lower lip.

I felt more than just a shiver. It was like a lightning bolt went through my entire body, and every part of me came to life. I slightly pulled back in shock of the feeling. "What was that?" I whispered into his lips.

"That was the mating bond. Your body is accepting it." He kissed me lightly again, "Next it will be your heart." He kissed me more fervently, "And finally, your mind will accept me as your mate." He pulled me tight against his body and kissed me until I could no longer breathe. It was everything I thought a kiss between two people in love should be, and nothing at all like what I experienced with my high school boyfriend.

He pulled away after a few minutes, but I wasn't ready to let him stop kissing me. I almost said something until I noticed his veins, they were pulsing red. No other colors, just red. "Are you okay? Your veins, I haven't seen them do that before. What's happening?"

He chuckled, then kissed my lips quickly and released me from his hold. For some reason, I started to feel cold. I already missed the warmth of his embrace.

"I am fine. The kissing was a little too intense for me. Sorry about that." He had the cutest smile when it was just the two of us. I think he might have saved that exact one only for me. When he smiled at me around others, it was not so warm and loving. This smile made me feel all warm and cuddly. I wondered if they had fireplaces on his planet. I thought about what it would be like on a cool night to cuddle in front of a fireplace with him and drink hot chocolate and share a blanket.

I looked up at him through my eyelashes. "Yes, that was very intense. But that doesn't mean I didn't enjoy it." I looked down and tried to hide the smile that wanted to take over my face.

"How long before you agree to be my mate? I don't know how much longer I can wait for you." He walked away from me, and heaved a sigh while running a hand through his gorgeous head of black hair.

"Venay, I know for you it's instant, but for me it's going to take more than a couple of days. Please give me some time to get to know you better. Maybe later tonight we can just talk and tell each other about our pasts and what we hope for in the future? You know, a normal dating type of conversation. Or at least that's what I think is normal. I haven't dated anyone since I left high school." I walked over and sat down on the couch, and he sat down next to me.

Right when we were comfortable, Venay received a message from his first officer. It was in their language, but I couldn't understand anything since I didn't have the universal translator installed yet.

While he was talking, I decided I wanted that done right away.

As soon as he was done talking I asked him, "Venay, can I

get the universal translator installed tomorrow? Would that be possible?"

He thought about it for a moment, "That might be a good idea. I think we should start the implantation immediately." He leaned forward and put his forearms on his knees. "There is something I want to tell you, but you can't tell any of the other humans, not yet. Can you keep a secret?"

"Yes, for now. But if it is something that will affect them, then I'll want them to know soon." I leaned forward and waited for his response. Keeping anything secret from my new friends was going to be tough, but if I could get Venay to open up and trust me, then it might be worth it to hold a few secrets, for now.

"That is fair." He stood up and paced between the window and the couch. I sat there waiting patiently while he collected his thoughts.

"That message, it was from my second in command, Eereen. He has picked up transmissions from an enemy ship that isn't far from us. We are watching them, but that ship shouldn't be anywhere near here." He stopped pacing and looked at me.

Before he continued, I noticed worry lines on his forehead and around his eyes. "Our two races don't get along, but we have had a long standing truce. This area is ours, and they are not to come into our territory. Once in a while we catch them here, and they usually run. But this time they aren't running. They are headed to a planet where we usually stop and pick up supplies on our way home. The planet only has an outpost that is manned by a few hundred warriors, their families, and some slaves. If they head any closer to that planet, we will have to stop them."

He came back and sat down next to me, "Do you understand what that means?"

"Do you have better weapons than they do?" I reached out

and took hold of his hand to offer my comfort and support to him. He seemed agitated.

"Our weapons should be greater than theirs, but we have heard some disturbing reports lately. They have somehow made a truce with another species and gained more advanced weaponry than what they had previously. This could be our first interaction with them and their new weapons. But don't worry, we are at least a day away from them. They could just be trying to mess with us. Some of their newer captains like to play games. But please be careful. If you hear any claxon bells ringing or see the red lights flash, stay where you are and find a way to keep yourself from getting injured. While we have a strong defensive shield, you could get jarred around and fall into something and hurt yourself if you are walking around. So please find a seat or someplace to strap yourself in." He cupped my cheek. While his touch was soft, his hand was calloused.

Even with the bad news, a sense of peace consumed me as he spoke.

"I will give you access to most areas of the ship but not to the bridge or to the holding cells. Most quarters will have emergency seats with straps, so if you are near living quarters, just put your hand to someone's ID lock. The occupant will open up for you and help you strap in. If no one is home, then you can override in an emergency. I will create a code for you to punch into the keypad. Can you do this for me? Stay safe if something happens?" Venay was agitated and all I wanted to do was help calm him down.

"Yes, I'll find a place to sit out the battle until you find me. But how will you know where I am?" I took his hand from my face and interlaced my fingers with his. My heart was pounding with the thought of having to endure a space battle. Me, a homeless girl in space preparing to fight a second alien species not long after learning that aliens really did exist. It was almost too much to process.

"Once you have the universal translator installed, I can just call you. It also serves as a communication device." He squeezed my hand.

"No tracker, right?" I raised my eyebrows and pursed my lips while considering that he just might lo-jack me.

He chuckled, "No, some masters do put tracking devices on their slaves, but most don't anymore. They rely on communicating with their slaves to find out where they are, when needed. And as my mate, you would never be subjected to a tracker."

"Do you think there is going to be trouble?" I bit my lip hoping it wouldn't come to a battle.

"I don't really know. I need to get to the bridge. Cazon will come back to get you shortly and help you and Lisa feed our guests. But remember, the men in Alpha cell block only get the rations, nothing else. Do you understand?" He lightly took hold of my shoulders and turned me to look directly into his eyes.

"Yes, of course. I agree that they are to be disciplined. This is the best punishment for them. And no worries, I'll stay away from the men. Cazon or one of the other guards will help Lisa feed them." I put one hand on his knee and squeezed it. For some reason I needed to touch him to assure myself as well as him. But I wasn't sure what I was assuring myself of.

He called Cazon who came immediately to get me.

CHAPTER ELEVEN

We walked over to Lisa's quarters and picked her up. "Lisa, have you heard? We get to have our universal translators installed tomorrow! Isn't that exciting?" Now I would be able to understand everything these guys said in front of me, no more wondering what they were discussing.

"We do? Rotna hasn't told me anything about that yet." She furrowed her brow.

"Oh, well I just talked Venay into it. Actually, it wasn't so much as talking him into it, as it was just asking him. And he said yes." I was giddy with excitement. While I was a bit leery about the procedure, I was excited to be able to eavesdrop on the warriors.

"How does it work, the procedure I mean?" Lisa smiled and waited for me to respond.

I stopped short and thought for a moment, "Oh, you know what? I didn't ask him. I just know that it is a subdermal implant behind our ear." I looked over to Cazon, "Do you know how the procedure works?"

He scratched his cheek, "Well, you have to be put under. I won't lie, you aren't going to feel all that great when you wake up. But the feeling should go away in a couple of hours.

We have pretty good medicine, at least compared to what you have on Earth." He smiled and motioned for us to follow him out of the room.

We made our way to the mess hall and prepared cheeseburgers for everyone except the Alpha cell men, well, and that idiot who hurt me in Beta. Most people were pretty happy with their dinners, and the men in the Beta cells really started to warm up to Lisa, at least. I still wasn't allowed to get near any of the men in either room. But that didn't matter to me, I was excited to see my friends ... and for tomorrow.

The men in Beta better appreciate this. Once Venay found out about that one guy who grabbed me, he almost gassed the whole room to punish them. But, I was able to talk him down and make him realize that only the one guy was an idiot, the rest of the men in there distanced themselves from that idiot. They shouldn't be penalized for the actions of one bad guy.

"Sheila, I'm going to be one of the first to get my universal translator installed tomorrow. You won't see Lisa or I tomorrow, but I hope to be fine by the next day." I was just too excited to keep the news to myself. There was a giddiness to my actions that hadn't been there for a long time. I think I even had a permanent smile glued on.

"Paris, what has gotten into you? Why would you want to be the first one to get that? Don't you know anything about alien tech? It could be a tracker or a death device of some sort! Haven't you seen any of the alien abduction movies?" Shelia shook her head an crossed her arms over her chest.

"Huh? No, I haven't seen any recent movies. What does a Hollywood movie have to do with real-life aliens and their technology?" I shrugged my shoulders and leaned in close to her, "This means that I will understand everything any of the warriors say." I raised my eyebrows while I waited for that to sink in.

I could see the moment realization dawned on her face, she stood back a bit and her mouth formed an O shape, and her eyebrows went up almost to her hairline. When she squeaked, she covered her mouth with her hand. "Oh, that is really smart!" Then she looked around as she realized how loud she said that.

She whispered, "Sorry."

"It's fine so don't expect us tomorrow. However, I do think Cazon will be spending more time with you while I'm away." I winked at her and sauntered off. She was going to have a nice day without me or Lisa getting in her way. That actually made it all the better. As much as I liked having Cazon around, I might want to ask Venay to assign someone else to my detail. Cazon needed more time with Sheila. She would jump at the chance to become his mate, but he needed to feel more comfortable with asking her. Only time spent together would do that.

✺

The next morning, I was up early and ready to go before Venay even came out of his room. To be fair, he was up really late the night before. I had been asleep for what seemed like a few hours before he finally came back and went to sleep.

He woke me up when he leaned over and kissed my forehead. "You know, you really could sleep in my bed, and I promise to keep my hands to myself."

I smiled up at him and kissed him back quickly on the lips.

"Hmm, I think I'm fine on the couch. Believe me, this is the most comfortable and luxurious bed I could ever ask for." I closed my eyes and started to fall back to sleep.

I heard him murmur, "One of these days, you are going to tell me your story."

My response was a sleepy, "Mm hmm." And the next thing I knew, it was morning, or what the ship simulated as morning.

I had noticed that the lighting around the ship changed to match the time of day. I guess that made sense. We were in space and time was not measured by the sun and the moon out here. So the lighting throughout the ship simulated a V'Zenian day, or so I was told by Cazon.

I was in the kitchen having my morning coffee and breakfast when Venay joined me.

I looked over the rim of my coffee mug as he walked in, and he smiled at me and said, "Good morning, sorry I woke you up when I came in late last night."

"No worries, something tells me that I'm going to have to get used to that. Do you work a lot of late nights?" I took a sip of the hot coffee the replicator had in its database. The rich brew was very tasty. It wasn't a peppermint mocha, but it still went down smoothly.

"Yes, I actually do. That is something I will have to work out with my staff now that you are here." He fixed himself coffee and breakfast and joined me at the table.

"How long will I be at the clinic today? Or what do you call your medical place here on ship?"

"We call it a med-bay. I think that is the closest English word for it. And I think you will be there for about six hours before you wake up, then a few more before I can take you home. I have a lot to do today, so while you are out I will be working on the bridge. But I have already instructed the doctor to call me when you wake up. I will come and visit you for as long as I can." He put a comforting hand on mine.

Thirty minutes later we were walking into their med-bay. I looked around and had to tell myself to close my mouth. It reminded me so much of a movie set. The colors were various hues of blue and silver, it was very comforting. The beds were a lot like what I had seen on some of my favorite sci-fi movies and TV shows growing up. I couldn't imagine them being comfortable, but when I sat on one, it was actually nice. I think it was like those funky beds with the model that puts a glass of wine on the bed, and then jumps up and down and the glass doesn't spill. Either way, I liked it.

An alien male came into the room and smiled at me. He was a hybrid, and his veins were pulsing many different colors of the rainbow. It was very soothing. He walked over to me and stuck his hand out, "Well hello, my name is Dr. Pleebs, it is nice to meet our Commander's mate."

I shook his hand. "Nice to meet you as well, and I'm Paris."

He smiled at me and bowed slightly to Venay. "Sir, she is in fine hands here. I will call you when she wakes up."

"Very well, but I would also like a call after the surgery, just to let me know everything went as planned." Venay's face hardened and I almost jumped.

It was kinda scary to see how he went from a loving, sweet man to a hardened Commander so quickly. But it was a good reminder of who he really was. And I wondered if the face he showed me was his real one, or if the battle-hardened alien male was his real side. I made a mental note to keep remembering I wasn't really his mate, I was his prisoner playing a game just to find a way home.

Dr. Pleebs bowed his head, "Of course, sir. As soon as I am done I will message you."

Venay came over, kissed my cheek, and said goodbye before heading out of the room.

The doctor explained the procedure to me and within a very short time I was falling asleep. One minute he was asking me to countdown from ten, and the next thing I knew, I was waking up in their version of a recovery room. But their version was so much nicer. They didn't have the drab egg shell colored walls that most hospitals on Earth did. Theirs was a very calm shade of green; it was like I was in the forest or something. One wall actually had a painting or wallpaper of some sort depicting a stream going through a bamboo garden. There was a slight sound, as I was waking up, I thought I might actually be next to a bubbling brook. Then as I fully came to I realized it was a soundtrack of some sort, like those alarm clocks in the fancy gadget stores in the mall. I was going to like this place.

It was about another hour before Venay was able to come see me. His face was covered in worry lines, and he wasn't really focused on me. He was a million miles away. Thankfully my translator had been tuned and was working before he came in because every time he spoke to me, it was in his language.

This was the weird part … I heard his guttural words and at first didn't understand, but after less than one second, it all made sense to me. If I didn't focus on his voice then I could follow along without a problem, but whenever I tried to focus on his voice, I would hear a combination of English and Klingon. I know they called their language something else, but it would always be Klingon to me.

"Venay, what's wrong? I know we haven't been together long, but I haven't seen you this worried before, nor have you ever spoken to me in your native language. Thankfully the translator is working fine. But what's going on?" I took a few deep breaths and started to worry that there was something bad happening. I wasn't in any pain but something in my chest tightened and ached.

He reached for my hand and held it in his big one. "That ship I told you about yesterday? It keeps flying close to our settlement and then away again. It is almost like it is trying to get my attention. I decided we must make sure that it doesn't get too close to our planet. They have no right to be here, and the inhabitants on that planet are more of the civilian type than actual warriors. They do have some training and munitions to help defend themselves, but they wouldn't do well against a ship with advanced weaponry. I have to assume they have the armaments our spies have seen, otherwise that captain is very stupid to try and goad me into a fight."

He let go of my hand and walked towards the door to my room and closed it. When he turned around, I could tell from the way his eyes were furrowed and the way he stood tall, erect, almost too tight, he was debating what to tell me.

"What else is it? Is everyone ok?" I could hear the worry in my own voice and tried to calm myself down.

"Yes, everyone is well. Lisa came out of her surgery just fine too. There are a dozen more women from your group who have gone through the process today as well, including Sheila. Somehow she and Cazon decided that it would be good if she did it today as well. But, I have asked the doctor to hold off doing anymore implants until we have dealt with this issue. I need the med-bay and all of his staff ready in case we do end up in a firefight with the enemy ship." He walked back toward me and sat on the edge of my bed.

"Venay, is there anything I can do to help? I should be up and about in a couple of hours. How far away are we now?" I sat up in the bed and Venay put a couple of pillows behind my back.

"We still have a few hours to go. By the time you are ready to go back to our quarters, we should be in reach of that planet. I have sent a message back to my admiral, and he has dispatched a couple of ships who are a few days away to come and join us. We will have back-up and that will help us to defend the planet. But I don't want you to do anything except stay in our quarters and rest. The doctor told me it could take a couple of days for you to feel one hundred percent. That chip in your head might do something to your equilibrium. Every human is different. Most have zero side effects, but there have been a couple of humans who had issues in the past." He relaxed a little bit, but then started pacing the small room.

Something inside of me wanted to calm him. "Well, let's just hope that none of us have any issues until we are all safe. I know you don't fully trust me, but would it be ok if I had some sort of weapon to use in case we are boarded?"

"If it comes to that, there will be a weapon provided to you, but until that time, I don't want you near anything that could cause you to get hurt." He eyed me curiously when he stopped his pacing.

"Meaning you don't trust me yet." I sighed as I realized he was too smart for my own good.

"No, it isn't that I don't trust you, it's just I don't want you to have to fight. You should never need to fight. That is my job, and when needed, my warriors'. We are here to protect you now." He slid his hand through my hair and caressed the side of my face with his hand.

This man had seen many years of hard work, his hands had multiple callouses on them. I think I even saw a scar from what looked like a long gash across his palm. Something told me he would protect me with everything he had and so would his warriors. I didn't doubt that at all.

"Ok, but as your mate, I would be making these trips with you right?" I leaned forward as I waited for his reply.

"Yes, of course." He bristled at the thought of leaving me behind on his planet.

"Then don't you think I should learn how to use a weapon in case we are ever in a fight with your enemy? What are they called?" I knew he couldn't argue with this.

"They are the Zateelians, and you may be right about the future. I will see to it that you are trained in hand to hand combat as well as with multiple weapons as soon as we get rid of the current situation." His face softened and my heart fluttered.

"Thank you. And just so you know, I'm pretty good at hand to hand combat. I took several years of self-defense classes. With living on the street at such a young age, I needed to use what I learned in those classes, a lot." I sat up straight and wanted him to know that I was no wilting flower. I could do my part in protecting the humans.

Part of me wondered if the other aliens would be worse than Venay and his group, or if they would be able to help us all get home, safely. However, the way Venay described their behavior had me a little bit worried about their intentions.

Would a good group of aliens attack us? Attacking the ship we were on could kill us all, so they may not be interested in helping us. Or, they could just be stupid. I decided to reserve judgement on the aliens until I knew more about them.

"For now, just focus on healing. Later we can discuss your training, okay?" He leaned down and kissed my forehead before standing up.

"Okay, for now." I narrowed my eyes. This discussion wasn't over. However, he was right in that I needed to heal from the procedure before I could join in any fighting. In fact, the excitement was making my stomach a bit queasy. Of course, I wouldn't tell Venay that, he'd probably make me stay in the med-bay even longer if he thought something was wrong with me. *I swear, he's worse than a mother hen.*

"I must get back to the bridge. Make sure someone calls me before you are ready to leave so that I can be the one to bring you back to our home." He took my hand once more and squeezed it.

I smiled. "I like that. It does feel like it could be my new home." I shook my head as I thought about what the future might hold for us. It had been so long since I had a real place to call home. Cardboard tents are not a home, just a hovel to survive in. Maybe this wouldn't be so bad after all. I had no one left on Earth. Well, except for Lola. Could I really do this, and enjoy this life with him? Or would playing up the mate role work enough to get me back to Earth? Did I still want to go back to Earth? *Of course, I do.*

My heart was turning out to be a traitor. It wanted to stay with Venay, but my mind and common sense would prevail. I just had to be strong and erect a cage around the bothersome organ that Venay was trying to claim.

I watched him walk out of the room, and then I worried about the other aliens until I fell asleep again.

At some point, someone came and woke me up to tell me I was fine and could go back to my quarters. The nurse told me that Cazon would escort me back since the Commander was too busy to come and get me. That hurt, but I kinda understood. We might be going to war anytime now. He should be on the bridge. Although, there was a tiny part of my heart that wanted Venay all to myself for just a little while. I hadn't felt real comfort from another soul in a very long time. It would have been nice if he could have been there for me.

"Cazon, I heard that Sheila got her implant today too. When did you two discuss that?" I asked as we walked toward my quarters.

"Last night, after you told her about yours. She asked me about it, so I suggested she get it done today as well. I think she is warming up to me and might say yes if I ask her to be my mate." A shy smile appeared on his face.

"Cazon, you are a ferocious warrior. Why are you so afraid to ask her to be your mate? I just don't understand this." I shook my head.

He stopped me when we were about halfway to my place. "Paris, I can handle anything that comes my way. Except for a woman. I have never been good with females. They usually take one look at me and run. I know that purebloods look very different from the hybrids, and it seems that is what the humans like. I have never had a human flirt with me or give me extra attention."

"Then why did you want a human for a mate?" His story had me curious as to what made him change his mind.

"Actually, I didn't. At least not at first. But I do want children. I want lots and lots of kids. A human mate is my best chance at that. Besides, I think that Sheila is my true mate. What do you call it? Soul mate?" He squinted at me and scratched his black hair.

Cazon was a good-looking warrior. He was tall, as were all of them. However, the purebloods looked to be even taller than the hybrids. While Venay was close to seven feet tall, I estimated Cazon to be over seven feet tall. His dark hair was wavy and long, for a male. In fact, most of the males tended to have longer hair. His was pulled back with a leather strap. His eyes were an interesting shade of blue that I hadn't seen before.

And as with all V'Zenian males I've seen so far, his veins pulsed different colors. Currently, his were pulsing blue. I was going to have to learn what the colors meant. Now that I took a closer look, his eyes matched the color of his veins, a deep blue similar to an Earth sky at dusk when the dark of night was coming quickly. I could see why Sheila thought he was good-looking, even if his skin tone was a purplish tint.

"Yes, soul mates. That is so sweet. But trust me when I say you need to man up and take her already. When she is ready to leave the med-bay, ask her to go home with you. She'll say yes. Just don't try anything inappropriate with her until after your mating ceremony." I chuckled as I thought about him trying to ask her. Oh, to be a fly on that wall. He would probably stammer and have trouble looking at her.

We started walking again and went the rest of the way in silence.

"Paris, will you be okay on your own? I would like to be there for Sheila. She is awake now, but I imagine it would be better if I were with her." Cazon turned his head toward the direction of the med-bay and I knew he was a goner.

I thought about how Venay was on the bridge the whole time, except for a few minutes, and realized that Cazon was really sweet. Sheila was one lucky woman. "Yes, of course, I'll be fine. Lisa loaned me a book, so I'll read that."

Cazon turned to walk away, and I stopped him, "Hey, Venay told me he has watched some old Earth movies and TV shows, is there a way for me to do that?"

"Of course, he hasn't shown you the Earth TV yet?" He had a puzzled look on his face.

"No, but we haven't spent much time together where we could have watched TV. He has pretty much told me the basics about what I need here, and we have talked about the current situation... with the uh, Zateelians." I whispered that word in case anyone was close by. He hadn't actually walked into my quarters yet, we were still chatting at my door.

To say he was shocked would have been an understatement. He gasped as his mouth fell open and then quickly ushered me into my quarters. "What did he tell you?"

"That we were most likely going to engage in some sort of battle with them. We're headed to a re-supply planet, and these enemies are basically playing chicken with us. So we might end up fighting. I'm surprised it didn't start while I was in surgery. He did tell me that no more procedures were going to be performed after today. He wants to wait until after he has dealt with that ship." I motioned for us to sit on the couch.

My body was quite tired. Must have been the effects of whatever they used to knock me out for the procedure.

He sat down at the other end of the couch. It was pretty comical because he always kept a discreet distance from me.

"Do you know what to do in case something happens?" Cazon had a very serious look on his face, and he was sitting up straight as a board. For someone who usually was happy and smiling, this was odd to see.

"Have you been keeping your emotions in check around me? I haven't seen you so serious before." I narrowed my eyes and waited for his response.

"Yes, I have. Now answer my question, please." He started to roll his shoulders and kept breathing in and out.

"I am to wait here in my quarters, unless he calls me or you come to get me. What's wrong, why are you so upset?" His nervousness was starting to wear off on me and I wondered if the situation was worse than what Venay had led me to believe.

"If they attack us, we should be able to fight them off… but should something happen, I need you to find a way to get over to Lisa's. You will be safer with her than here, in the Commander's quarters. If the enemy finds you here, let's just say they will either kill you, or take you as prisoner. You don't want them taking you as prisoner." He shivered.

"Stink, you think they might get on this ship, don't you?" I started breathing heavily and worry began to take over. Venay had definitely not told me everything.

"I can't rule out the possibility." He tried to smile, but it didn't reach his eyes.

"Then give me a weapon, something to defend myself with. I won't turn it on you guys. I am beyond that now. Please trust me." I pleadingly looked at him, while wringing my hands.

He heaved a heavy sigh, "Alright, I will show you where you could possibly find a weapon, but only get it and use it as a last resort. The best thing is to wait with Lisa. I am going to tell Sheila the same thing if she comes home with me."

Cazon stood up, and I followed him into the kitchen.

"If we are attacked, all of the living quarters will be unlocked for you. However, no one can get in without the proper access, but all of the mates will be able to get out if they need to. And you will want to leave this room as quickly as you can. The Zateelians will want you as leverage against the Commander." He walked over to the cupboard.

He opened it up and took his Taser out of his belt and put it in the back of the top shelf. "Come grab this if you need it, and then run to Lisa's. You should all be safe there. I doubt they will look at regular crew quarters, not at first anyway. Just be very careful you don't shoot any of us with it, ok?" He closed the door and motioned for me to follow him back to the living room.

"Of course, I don't want to hurt you guys. Most certainly not while enemy aliens are boarding this ship. That would be very stupid." Unless they seemed like they might be attacking us to save the humans. But that was starting to seem less likely. The more time I spent with the V'Zenians, the more I believed they were the better choice. At least for now.

As we sat back down on the couch, I yawned, and my stomach growled at the same time. The gurgling from my stomach was even louder than normal due to my mouth being open from the yawn.

Cazon chuckled and stood back up, "Alright, I am heading back to my mate. I suggest you eat something and then get some sleep. Tomorrow just might be a really crazy day. If that ship doesn't leave this system by tomorrow, we will have no choice but to open fire on them. You will need to be ready for that."

I put a hand on his shoulder before he walked to the door, "Thank you, Cazon. You have been a great friend these past few days. I just want you to know that I really appreciate everything you have done for me up to this point."

"Hey now, don't go saying goodbye. I know nothing bad is going to happen to you, but I want you prepared in case the worst-case scenario does happen. It's just me being prepared, that is all." He walked toward the door and looked over his shoulder at me and smiled as he walked out.

"I really do hope I see him again, and that those aliens just leave the system now that we are much closer to them," I mused as I walked to the kitchen to make dinner for one. It was getting late and I still hadn't heard from Venay.

After dinner, I took a shower and got ready for bed. The drugs hadn't worn off completely, and I was too tired to wait up for Venay.

It couldn't have been more than a few minutes after I fell asleep when I felt him sit next to me on the couch. "You should sleep in the bedroom, I will sleep out here on the couch. That way if I need to get up in the middle of the night I won't wake you." He leaned down and kissed me lightly on the lips.

"No, this is much better. You need the sleep more than I do. And somehow I doubt your big frame would fit on this couch very well." I pulled my hand out of the blanket and rubbed his arms. For some reason, I felt like I needed to touch him. Once I did have my hand on him, I felt pressure coming off my back and shoulders, almost like I had been carrying a heavy load, and now he took it away from me.

He smiled before he leaned down and gave me an even better kiss. This time he laid down on the couch with me partially underneath him while he continued to kiss me. I put my right hand in his hair, something I had wanted to do for a while now. I grabbed a handful and pulled him closer to me while my other hand made its way to his lower back.

He used both of his arms to prop himself up so he wasn't crushing me with his body weight. The level of kissing was growing hotter and more intense as the minutes passed. I had never felt this close to any man before, and I wanted to be closer still. I pulled him as tight to myself as I could and a small moan escaped from his lips.

Venay started to slow the kiss down, and then eventually pulled away, and my warmth went with him. "When this business with the Zateelians is over, will you be ready to become my mate?" He whispered in my ear, and it sent chills down my spine.

I couldn't think. All I wanted was for his lips to be back on mine, but my mind was registering what he said even as my heart was chastising me for letting his lips get away. "Yes." That was all I could think to say as I grabbed the back of his head and pulled him back to me for another kiss.

He gave into my desires, but stopped me when it started to get heated again. "I am so sorry, but I can't kiss you like this and not cross that line." He looked into my eyes and used his left hand to caress my cheek. The next thing I knew he was peppering my face with soft kisses, and I heard him moan, but it was more of an angry moan.

He immediately stood up and walked a short distance away from the couch. "Paris, you tempt me too much. It is probably a good thing we are not sharing a bed yet. I doubt I would get any sleep if you were next to me."

I smiled and looked up into his face and knew he was going to be my mate. And I wanted it soon. Although, this seemed to be happening too quickly. Maybe that mating bond thing Venay talked about was real after all? "How soon do you think we could arrange the ceremony?" I sat up on the couch and patted the seat next to me.

He shook his head, "I can't sit next to you and not touch you, Paris. The only way to keep in control is for me to stand over here." He ran his hand through his hair, and I watched as his biceps flexed. All I wanted to do was touch his arms. "But I think we could arrange it in about a week, or less. Once we get rid of the Zateelians, I think we should have our ceremony on the planet. They have some of the most beau-tiful gardens I have ever seen. It would be the perfect place for our mating ceremony. Then we could spend a night in one of their mountain cabins. Just the two of us, with no one to disturb us."

It sounded so romantic. Was he a closet romantic? Cuz

that would be nice. By day he seemed to be this strong, steely warrior, and by night a soft, cuddly teddy bear? That would work for me … best of both worlds.

"I like it, a lot. It's time. Let's make those plans Venay." My heart was fluttering thinking of what it would be like to marry him and one day to have his children. My thoughts were just about to turn to something else, when he turned around and headed to his room.

It all seemed to be happening so fast. It wasn't too long ago I wanted to use him to find a way to get back to Earth. Now, my heart was telling me to let him love me. *What was wrong with me?*

He called out, "Goodnight my mate," over his shoulder and closed his bedroom door.

My heart flipped again, and I wondered if we could we have the perfect family while flying through space with me supporting him in his mission. *Hold up. That won't work for me.* I could not support abducting more humans. Marrying him was what my heart was calling for. However, if we did marry, I couldn't support him in his job.

It seemed as though my heart and my mind were not in sync.

I released a heavy sigh and laid back down and tried to go to sleep, but my mind wouldn't shut off.

There had to be a way to help his people and not hurt mine in the process. But, first things first, we had to get through tomorrow.

CHAPTER TWELVE

The next morning brought nothing but dread and nerves. I must have slept very lightly, because for the first time I heard Venay get up and get ready. He never made noise in the morning, or if he did, I couldn't hear it.

While I was laying on the couch thinking about today, he walked out of his room all ready. He looked at me but only gave me a tentative smile and a soft, "Good morning." Normally he came over to my couch and sat down. We would speak a bit, and he usually kissed me. But not today. He looked to be all warrior, and no mate.

I got up and followed him into the kitchen, "Are you heading to the bridge?"

"Yes, how are you feeling today? No side effects from the procedure?" Venay didn't even look at me as we spoke. He was focused on what he was doing.

"I'm just fine. Sleep wasn't as good as normal, but with everything going on, I'm not surprised." I shrugged my shoulders and fixed myself a cup of coffee. Before I left our quarters I would most likely need another cup.

I still didn't know what to do about marrying him, since I can't marry someone whom I can't support. His job was really the only thing causing me to be unsure. I did feel that mating bond. It was the only thing that explained how my heart had changed so quickly. However, his work in the slave trade was a major issue for me.

But we still had a tense situation to get through first, and I certainly couldn't tell him my doubts in case he went into battle today. *He has to believe I am behind him 100% today.* Hopefully, when this mess was over with, I could talk some sense into him.

He fixed himself something that resembled a protein shake. Normally, he fixed me an Earth breakfast, and he ate it with me. But today he was all business, even in his food choices.

"What is that?" I pointed to his tall, clear cup that had a straw in it. The ingredients didn't look too appetizing. It was a puke green color of sloshy liquid. Not something I wanted to try.

"It is a healthy protein substitute. I need something that will metabolize quickly today, and this is usually what I have when I prepare to go into battle. That ship is coming back around, we will intercept him in less than 3 hours. Please stay here in this room today, unless I or Cazon instruct otherwise, okay?" He took my hand and brought it to his lips.

I couldn't help but smile as he worried over my safety. "I need to feed the people in your holding cells. But after that I will come back here. Don't worry about me. I'll be fine."

"That is fine, but do not tell them what's going on. Maybe you can leave them some protein meal replacement bars. We use them when we go down to planets for a few days, just in case we can't find any local foods to our liking or dietary requirements."

"Actually, that's a great idea. Thanks." I smiled and kissed him on his cheek before he left the room.

As I started to make my breakfast, he came back in and grabbed me for a warm and solid hug. "I love you, I hope you know that. I will do whatever I have to in order to make sure you are safe, do you understand?" His whispered words sent chills up my spine.

I pulled back from his warm chest and looked up to his eyes. I had yet to see him cry, but in that moment, I knew I never wanted to see him do so. The look on his face was enough to bring me to tears. His eyes, with those enticing violet irises, were teary. He had such a sad expression on his face. I wanted nothing more than to hold him and kiss away his worries.

Frown lines were forming and getting bigger. It had me worried. "I know you will take care of me, don't worry about me. You have an entire ship to take care of. I will be here or at Lisa's, once we are done feeding everyone in the holding cells. Please focus on your work today and not me." I gave him a tentative smile and kissed him one last time before he left our quarters.

I sat down at the table after he left and thought about what just happened. This seven-foot giant of an alien was possibly about to go into battle with a ship that shouldn't have the ability to hurt us, but most likely did. And, he was more worried about me than the rest of the inhabitants on his ship. I hung my head and scratched the back of my neck. *He really does love me, doesn't he?*

Before my breakfast was finished, Cazon showed up. But my appetite was pretty much gone anyway. I was nervous but not for myself. I was more nervous for Venay, and for my people locked up in cells with no way to protect themselves if we were boarded.

"Cazon, what would happen to the humans if we were overtaken by the Zateelians?" I didn't even take the time to great him a proper good morning.

He took a deep breath and huffed out, "Nothing good, that's for sure." Then he hurried out of my quarters, and I had to almost run to catch up to him. He kept a really fast pace and before I knew it, we were at Lisa's door.

He pushed her doorbell, and we waited in the hallway for her.

"Cazon, please tell me. I need to know. Will they be killed or left alone?" I bit my lower lip worrying about everyone's safety.

He scratched his head, "Neither, they will be taken as slaves to the Zateelian's home world. But it won't be any better than my home. In fact, they will wish they were back here in their cells eating that, what did you call it? Chalky, jello mold?"

"Will they, um, will... they try and force the women to mate with them?" I couldn't think of anything worse to happen to us.

"No, they are more insectoid then humanoid, so there isn't compatibility between the two species, thankfully." His face darkened and knew there was more he wasn't telling me.

The door swooshed open, and Lisa came out.

"Hey there, why the sad faces?" She looked between both of us.

"Oh, it's nothing. I was just wondering who was going to mate next? Any ideas?" I didn't want to worry Lisa. We all had enough on our plates, plus I wasn't sure how much she knew about the situation.

Cazon stood up proud with the biggest smile I have ever seen on him. "Last night, Sheila came home with me to be my mate."

Lisa and I both squealed with excitement. "Oh, how did you ask her? And what did she say?" Lisa and I both blurted out questions to him without really giving him a chance to answer.

It would be nice to have another woman in our group to talk with, and hopefully walk around freely with.

He backed up a bit and held his hands up in front of him, "Whoa, wait a minute. Give me a break. I don't do hysterical female speak." He stopped moving when his back hit the wall across from Lisa's door.

"Sorry about that this is just exciting for us! Where is Sheila? Why isn't she helping us?" I looked at Cazon and narrowed my eyes at him, he was up to something.

"She, well, I decided she needed to stay in our room today. I wanted to make sure she gets plenty of rest." The big alien warrior wasn't looking me in the face.

I knew what he was up to, "Cazon, you want to protect her don't you? You have locked her up so she can't be near me today, haven't you?"

He looked between the two of us, "She doesn't know." Then turned his eyes toward Lisa.

"What don't I know?" Lisa asked as she looked back and forth between Cazon and me.

I didn't care if got in trouble, Lisa needed to know exactly what was going on. It would probably upset her, but how could she be prepared if she didn't know? "We might have to fight off an alien ship who has tried to play chicken with us for the past couple of days. Venay is worried they might have the arsenal to hurt this ship, badly. If we end up in a firefight today, I am supposed to come to your room and stay with you. I was hoping that all of us women would stay together."

"Wait, what? We might have to fight another alien species?" She put one hand on her hip and the other on her forehead, like she was getting a headache, or mad. Probably mad.

"Well, at least we have a good shot at beating them." I was trying to be optimistic, not just for Lisa, but for myself too. There was too much going on, just as I was starting to adjust to my new life and maybe even accept it, we had to deal with an eminent attack. We all needed optimism.

Cazon ushered us towards the mess hall, "Ok, so no one

says anything about this to the guests in our cells, got it?" He eyed us both once we looked back at him.

"Of course, I have no desire to start another panic with the *guests* as you eloquently put it." Part of me wanted to keep calling them prisoners, abductees, but another was almost ready to refer to them as slaves, and that part of my brain was scaring the tar out of me.

We quietly made the breakfast as quickly as we could. While we were in the last room, which was Alpha room, things got dicey.

"Huh, sounds like…" All of a sudden we heard a really loud banging sound, and then it felt like we hit something. Everyone who had been standing fell down on the ground.

As I stood up and looked around, I noticed that Cazon had a very worried look on his face. "Alright, everyone sit down and hold on to the bars, we are going to be flying through some very tough space. Paris and Lisa, come with me, now."

Lisa and I looked at each other and started to follow Cazon. Natalie called out to me, "Paris, what's going on? Did we hit something?"

"I really don't know. But do as Cazon says. I gotta get going. Please stay safe everyone." I yelled that last bit out over my shoulder as I ran to catch up to Cazon.

As soon as we stepped into the hallway, the ship rocked again and we all fell into the wall. We stayed upright, but just barely.

We ran to Lisa's quarters and Cazon handed me his laser pistol, "Do you know how to handle one of these?"

"Is it just point and shoot?" The weapon was lighter than I expected, and my hand fit around the handle well enough. Even though my hands were so much smaller than the aliens.

He snorted, "Yeah, pretty much." He handed me the pistol and had me point it at the wall but kept my finger off the trigger.

"Do you see the sight guide?" He asked.

"Yes." Then I lined up the guide from the back of the gun to the dot on the end of the barrel.

"Yes, just like that. Keep those two marks lined up and aim for the chest. Pull the trigger like you would an Earth gun, but don't hold it down. This type of weapon only shoots out short bursts of energy," Cazon instructed.

"Ok, thanks. Now go, do whatever it is you do when you have to defend this ship. And kill all of those idiots!" I was getting a taste of bloodlust, and I liked it. Maybe I would get a chance to use this weapon? No, wait. That would mean we were losing, and they found a way to get on this ship. That wouldn't work.

Not two minutes after Cazon left, Venay called me on my communicator that was implanted with the translator. "Venay! Are you ok?"

"I am fine, how are you? Where are you? I called our room, and you didn't answer." He sounded really worried, and I could hear the warriors in the background yelling orders, and then we were hit again. Thankfully Lisa and I were sitting on the ground. We were both sitting back against the couch in the living room with a good view of the door.

"I'm fine. Lisa and I are in her quarters. Cazon just left us here. Don't worry about us, you get back to work and save us." I decided the other aliens had to be bad if they attacked us in V'Zenian space without any provocation. That is if everything Venay had told me was true, and I was starting to believe it was.

"Stay where you are. Don't go anywhere. They are trying to blow a hole in the ship. I'm sure they want to try and board us. Tell no one who you are if they do get on board. Stay with Lisa. Now I wish I would have given you a weapon." I could hear the anger and frustration in his voice.

"Venay, I have a weapon. Cazon left his laser pistol with

me. We are going to be fine. You just focus on squishing every single one of those insectoids, so I don't have to!" Even though Cazon told me they were insectoid, I had no clue how large they were. I really hoped I wasn't going to find out, either.

"I knew you were perfect for me. I love you, and I will see you soon." His warm voice strengthened me, and I was looking forward to seeing him once they defeated the Zateelians.

My heart was expanding, and I knew I had very strong feelings for him, but love? *Not yet.* "Venay, you better make it back to me so we can have that romantic wedding on the planet you promised me. And more importantly, our honeymoon in the mountains. Now hang up this call or whatever it is and get to work!"

"Yes ma'am!" I heard him start to give an order, and then our communication was cut off. The fact that he called me right in the middle of a battle warmed me through, but he shouldn't have done that. If we made it out of this, I was going to tell him to never call me again during battle, unless he had orders for me. I needed him focused on killing the enemy and protecting the ship, not me.

CHAPTER THIRTEEN

My heart was still pumping an hour later, and my adrenaline seemed to be burning out. I was exhausted just sitting there holding tight to the laser gun as well as to the couch every time our ship was hit. I wanted to say that I could hear the laser cannons fire, or whatever they called them on this ship. But I knew it must be my imagination creating the sounds in order to keep track of the fighting somehow.

However, I really did hear some of the torpedoes going back and forth. It was a weird sound, almost like Superman flying super-fast through a tunnel and taking all sound with him through that tunnel. Then it was super quiet for less than half a second, which was always followed by a loud bang, and then the ship would jerk one way or another. At least there was a warning sound before the torpedoes hit. They packed the most punch.

The next hit, well, it was almost what killed us. The ship started to tilt, like it had lost its stabilizers or something, but we must have gotten a good hit on them as well because another hit didn't come for a while. I could feel us limping along. Since we were slanted, Lisa and I had to hold on tight to the couch. I had never been so happy to see furniture tied to the ground before. Some of the knickknacks and loose items like chairs and pillows were flying around as we tried to get away from the enemy ship.

We turned and headed to something, at the time I didn't know what. But at least we weren't getting shot at any more. It seemed like days before we made it to the planet. The only reason I knew we were at the planet is because Venay called me, again.

"Venay, I'm fine. No need to worry about me," I stated before he could even greet me.

"Thank the moons! But I am calling to warn you, this next bit is going to get very difficult. There should be a place in the quarters you are in where you can strap yourself to a fold down chair on the wall. Find that and get your butt in it now. We are going to try landing this ship on the planet before the enemy can catch up to us. But with the damage, re-entry is going to make for a very bumpy flight. Can you do that?"

"Yes, I can. Thank you, Venay." Okay, so his calling me was a good idea. I would never have known I needed to strap in if he hadn't, or where the chair was to strap in.

He grunted and then hung up. "Lisa is there a set of fold down emergency chairs that we can lock ourselves into? You know, like the jump seats on a commercial flight?"

"Yes, in the back bedroom. There are two seats there. What's going on?" She took one hand off the couch and flexed it before switching hands and doing the same thing.

"What did Rotna say when he called you?" I wanted to ask her but Venay called me only a few moments later.

"He tried to tell me what was going on, but was told to focus on his task, not his mate." Her cheeks actually turned a shade of pink. I wondered when they were planning their ceremony.

"Glad to know he's fine." I looked around for the entrance to the back room.

We both stood up and tried to level ourselves before moving.

"Why do we need to do this? Is the ship getting worse?" Lisa asked, with wide eyes.

"Yes, we're approaching the planet and going to attempt to land before the enemy ship can catch us. The re-entry is going to be tough." I wobbled around as we headed to the emergency seats.

We made it to the back room and found the seats. There were a few things that had blocked our way, but we moved them without much issue.

It was a good thing Venay called to warn me, because we weren't even buckled in when I felt the ship jerking and shaking like an amusement park ride about to go off the rails.

My teeth hurt so bad within just the first two minutes, I thought they might all be cracked, first from the chattering they were doing with the way we jumbled around and then from the pressure I put on my mouth to stay closed. Somewhere along the way I had bit my tongue and it hurt.

I couldn't say how long it took for us to get through the atmosphere, but it felt like forever. I could tell when we made it because we started to smooth out and the ship wasn't jerking so badly. The loud noise that almost made me deaf had also quieted down, now it was more like a ball whistling through the air. Although, my head was pounding and my body ached from all of the jostling and clenching. I don't think I have ever held on to anything as tightly as those restraints, ever.

"Lisa, you ok?" I rubbed my neck and hoped the worst was over.

"Did we make it?" She looked around the room wide eyed and I could see she had been crying. Her face was streaked with the paths her tears left.

But I couldn't blame her. I was pretty scared myself and if

I hadn't survived five years on the streets I would have probably been crying as well.

"So far. I don't think we have landed yet. So stay seated until we are told we can move. I have a feeling we are going to feel the landing as well." I stretched out my arms while the ride was somewhat smooth and worked the tight muscles.

The ship was still tilted, and the seats were very uncomfortable. We were slanted to the left so the belts that made up the restraints were digging into my left side. It felt like one of those carnival rides where you went around in circles, but you were hanging on one side, and the ride seat was digging into your entire side. It was similar to that, but worse. I figured I would have bruises later on and hoped that would be the worst of it.

"Lisa, tell me about the plans you and Rotna have made for your wedding. When do you want it to take place?" She looked like she might get hysterical any moment. Her eyes were all over the place, and she was having trouble breathing. She didn't look injured, unless the belts did something internally.

"Huh? What? Oh, yea, wedding. Ummm, we spoke about it last night. We agreed that we wanted it to happen as soon as we could get some time on the Commander's schedule. Do you think he will have time tomorrow?" She was dazed. I wasn't sure she understood what was happening. How could she if she was thinking Venay could marry them tomorrow, after crash landing on a planet while in a firefight with a heavily armed enemy ship?

"Lisa, do you know what just happened?" I wished at that moment I could get out of my seat, but I knew there was no way it would be safe until after we made landing.

"Yes, we are landing on a planet." Lisa's voice was monotone and her gaze was distant, like she was focused on the stars, but we couldn't see outside since it was an inside room.

"Because we just got our butts kicked in a firefight with an enemy ship. There won't be time to get married, not at least for a while. I couldn't even tell you how long it will take to fix our ship. Or if the Zateelians will come for us. Lisa, I need you to focus. Can you do that?" Her eyes were still glazed over, and her mouth was hanging open. She kept moving her head like she was listening to some music somewhere.

Just then I got a communication from Venay, "Paris, are you ok?"

"Yes, both Lisa and I are ok. She might have some internal injuries, but I think she's alright. However, she appears to be in shock. How much longer before we land?" All I wanted in that moment was to be on the ground, safe and sound.

"We came in too fast, so I have to keep her flying as long as possible to slow down, which means we won't be close to the settlement here. They will come for us and help us soon. Stay in your seats. Don't move until I tell you, okay?"

"Of course, I'm betting we will feel it when we land, won't we?" I winced thinking about the jarring pain we were about to experience.

"Yes, I am afraid you will. And Paris, don't say anything, but Rotna is hurt, badly. Lisa might know. If he called her before he went unconscious then she knows. Don't say anything until we land, and you can check her out." Venay's voice lost a little bit of his Commander tone and I sensed the worry for his warrior.

It made me worry for Rotna as well. "Ok, thank you. Um, any news about the enemy ship? Are they following us?"

He sighed, and I knew it was bad, "Yes, they are heavily damaged, but they did make it through. However, they are not very close to us. They will have to crash land as well so we should have some time before they come looking for us or the settlement. I just hope that they aren't able to crash very close to the outpost."

"Thank you for being honest with me. You have no idea how much that means to me. I still have the gun Cazon gave me. Once we land, where should I take Lisa?" I needed to put my emotions to the side and focus on the task at hand. We were in an emergency situation. While it was different from what I had experienced living on the streets, I was still used to ignoring my emotions and focusing on how to get out of a bad situation. That was pretty much daily life for me … before.

It looked like my life really didn't improve much. Sure, the food was better, as was the bed, but life might be more dangerous living with aliens. I missed my dog.

"Stay where you are. I will let you know where to go once we land. Please don't try to leave your room until you hear from me. The ship will be unstable, and I still have no idea where the Zateelians will land."

"Right, oh, then I guess you better get back to work. And Venay, thank you for checking in on me so much. I know you have a huge responsibility with the entire ship."

"You're welcome, Paris. See you soon."

That man, or alien, was stealing my heart without even trying. All he had to do was show me love and attention, and my stupid heart was falling for him. I still couldn't get over the slave issue. I didn't want to fall completely for him and then end up accepting slavery. It wasn't right. However, my heart wouldn't stop its erratic beating for him. I was truly afraid that I would end up head over heels in love with this great big warrior before this was all over with.

The cage I thought I had around my heart seemed to be breaking up.

The ship started to lurch and leaned to the left and then to the right. We had begun the crash. There was no way this ship was going to survive intact after this crash. We bumped up, and then down and we even spun a bit. My stomach was not happy. It was a gurgling mess, and I had never been so happy to have a mostly empty stomach before. It had to have been at least four or five hours since I ate breakfast, so there wasn't much in my stomach to worry about.

The noise was so loud and harsh that my ears started to ring. It sounded like the ship might be breaking apart. We were being jerked so harshly that I wouldn't be surprised if it broke up in a couple of pieces. Just then the ship jumped up. The reason I knew we jumped up was because my stomach was all over the place. Just like in a roller coaster ride where when you get to the top of the highest point in the track, then go over the cliff and start to go down, and you lose your stomach. Well, that was what it was like, except the straps caused pain. We bounced up high, and then all of a sudden, we dropped like a roller coaster ride.

When we hit the ground, my whole body jarred and my teeth clicked together so harshly, I knew I had cracked a tooth this time. Thankfully I kept my tongue glued to the roof of my mouth so I didn't bite it again.

My head was throbbing, not just an ache, but an actual throb. I could feel my pulse through my head and it was going a mile a minute. I couldn't feel my body at first, and I didn't know exactly what happened. Like in a car accident, it all occurred so fast. My eyes seemed to be covered with something black, but as I opened and closed them, my vision started to return. However, my seat had come loose from the wall, and I was on top of the bed in a very uncomfortable position with the seat on my back and my face smooshed in the mattress. I tried to roll to my side, but it took me a few attempts before I turned over.

Once I was on my side I looked around the room. Even though most of the furniture was locked down, it looked like a tornado ripped through here. The dresser had come undone and was right next to the bed I was on. Anything that had been loose was spread all over the room. From my angle I couldn't see Lisa, and I didn't hear her either.

My hands hurt from holding on so tightly to the straps
that it was an effort to get my fingers to open. I had to
stretch them out a bit before I tried to undo the straps. Once
they were undone, I fell to my stomach on the edge of
the bed.

"Lisa? Lisa you okay?" I called out in a raspy voice, but got
no response.

I hoped she was alright. The first thing I needed to do was
get up and stretch my tightly constricted muscles. They had
tightened up and some locked in place while I was being
thrown about like a rag doll during the crash. I wanted
nothing more than to have Venay come and get me and hold
me. But that couldn't happen anytime soon. He had the
entire ship to think about. And besides, chances were pretty
good that our ship had broken apart. I had no idea how long
it would take him to get here, or even if he could.

After about a minute or two of stretching on the bed,
everything seemed to work fine, no broken bones at least. So
I stood up and looked over toward the wall were my seat had
been, and Lisa's seat was barely hanging on. She appeared to
be passed out, at least that was what I was going with. Her
eyes were closed, not open with a vacant stare, so I assumed
she was still alive. Living on the streets you come across
quite a few dead bodies. The one thing they all had in
common, was the vacant stare in their eyes. That stare is
what you remembered for the rest of your life. Not how nice
or how mean that person was, just how they looked when
you found them dead.

"Lisa, answer me if you can." I climbed over a few things
to make my way to her.

I felt her neck for a pulse. It was weak but there. Then I
started to feel her body for broken bones. Her arms and legs
seemed alright. There was a place on her stomach that
worried me. It was where the seatbelt was digging in, and I
lifted her shirt to see a huge bruise already forming. I didn't

know what that meant but pretty sure she had some internal damage.

I looked around for something soft to put below her. She was going to fall off that seat once I unlocked her restraints. I didn't want her falling on the ground.

There really wasn't anything to help cushion her fall, so I grabbed the bedding and pulled hard. The seat I had been in was pretty heavy and still atop the bed, so I had to work hard to get the sheets and blankets off. Then I found the pillows on the other side of the room and put them all below her. I slowly undid her buckles. My hands were still quite sore from holding onto my belts.

Before I undid the last buckle, I reached around her chest to try to hold her a bit before she fell like a lump to the ground. I wasn't very strong so once I got that last belt, we both fell, but I cushioned her fall a with my own body. "Lisa, are you awake?" I asked as I moved the hair from her face.

I whispered in her ear, "Lisa, Rotna is alive, and he needs you. Please wake up, I can't carry you."

I dragged her closer to the dresser so that I could hold her head in my lap while I leaned back against it.

She wasn't awake, but at least she was alive. I sat there thinking about what I should do when I heard a beep in my ear. It was an incoming communication! "Venay, is that you? Are you ok?"

"Yes, sweetheart, I am fine. How are you? Are you hurt?" I could hear the relief in his voice as it went lower and softer.

"Oh, thank the stars! I'm okay, a bit sore and a few scrapes, but I'm fine. Lisa's another story. She's alive but passed out and injured. I don't know what to do for her." My shoulders slumped and I sighed in relief. Venay was alive.

"There should be a med-kit somewhere in her quarters, most warriors keep them in their bathrooms. Check there or the kitchen, but please be careful. We have stopped, but I don't know if the ship will stay steady or not. She broke up as we crashed." At least he was still being honest with me.

"I figured as much. How long before you can get to me?" I was done being strong, I wanted my warrior.

"I honestly don't know. I can't leave the bridge yet. We are getting reports of multiple injuries as well as a few deaths. And honey, the ship broke up close to the holding cells. I don't know how the humans are doing. We are trying to get some warriors over there, but it is slow going."

I could hear the sadness in his voice and felt his pain. This was not going to be good. It didn't matter that the aliens saw them as slaves, it was going to be hard on the entire crew if we lost those people.

"Okay, once I get Lisa stable, I'll go and check on them. I'm not too far away. That could be why our room is so torn up. If we were really close to where the ship broke up, the structural integrity of our area of the ship must have gone past its limits. My safety seat actually came off the wall, but I landed on the bed. Lisa's was barely hanging on. I think she might have internal damage from the seat belt. She's badly bruised on her stomach. Do you think the medical crew could send someone here to look at her?" The only reason I suspected internal damage from the seatbelt was because of high school friend of mine had been in a car accident and had similar issues. Her liver was damaged, but she did recover, thankfully. So I was confident with the right medical help Lisa would be fine, too.

"Call the Doctor and ask him to add her to the list to triage, but you might be waiting a while. Most of the ship is out of power, so the doors will have to be manually opened as you move about the ship. But don't go too far, if you can't easily get around something, ok? I don't want you to get stuck somewhere." He sighed and I could imagine him running a hand across his face as he spoke to me.

"Ok, how do I call the doctor? Or you for that matter? I only know how to answer a call."

"Push the spot under your ear where they put your translator and say, 'Paris to the doctor,' and if he doesn't answer then try the comm unit on the wall to contact the med-bay. If that doesn't work call me back, and I will see if I can reach any of the nurses."

"Alright, I can do that… Venay?" My voice broke when I spoke his name.

"Yes, Sweetheart?" His silky voice was calm, and I appreciated it.

"I… I want to see you. I know I need to be strong, but at the moment, I'm afraid." Tears stung my eyes. "How long before I can see you?" I took a couple of deep breaths, and tried to not cry, but a tear ran down my cheek. The fear was much stronger than the physical pain.

"You are strong Paris. You can do this. If you don't want to check on the humans, then make your way to the bridge if you can. You might not make it this far. I think the ship is broken up somewhere between the bridge and the living quarters. The holding cells would be in the middle of the ship. So, call me back after you check on your humans, and then we will see if there is a route you can take to get to me." His voice was strong and in command. I knew he was worried about me, but he was the Commander and would lend his strength to anyone in need.

"Okay and thank you. I will be strong. I can do this." I started to repeat in my head over and over my new mantra for the day, *I can do this, I am strong and independent, I don't need Venay to rescue me.*

After he said goodbye, I went looking for the emergency medical kit and kept saying my mantra over and over. I found it in the kitchen and made my way back to the bedroom. The entire place was an absolute mess. I had to crawl over a few pieces of furniture that came loose in the crash, but it wasn't too difficult.

I did make a call to the doctor, and he said he would send someone soon. There were a lot of injured on this ship. So, for the moment, all Lisa had was me.

CHAPTER FOURTEEN

When I made it back to her, she was no different. I opened up the med-kit and had no clue how to use the items inside. One thing looked like it might be some sort of scanning device, based on watching sci-fi movies. So I took that out and pushed buttons. It turned on and in a language I couldn't read, gave instructions. Great! I kept pushing buttons just in case it had audio too. It did! My universal translator told me to put the device over the injured area, and then push the yellow button and hold.

Turns out I was right, she had liver damage. But the device told me what to do next. There was another gadget in the med-kit that looked like it was a tablet. I put the electronic device over her stomach, and it emitted a low level blue glow around the edges. I heard a whirring sound and hoped that meant it was working.

While that was doing its thing, I cleaned my wounds with the antiseptic spray I found in the kit and some cotton balls. It smelled just as bad as antiseptic cleaner back home. My nostrils burned and I coughed a few times.

What was I going to do with Lisa? I needed to check the holding cells, but there was no way Lisa was going to be able to go with me. As I sat there contemplating my next move, Lisa stirred.

"Lisa! You're awake. How do you feel?" I jumped to her side and hope filled my heart.

She started to move and noticed the tablet on her stomach and tried to move it.

I reached out to her to stop her, "Don't touch that, it's a medical device that's healing your injuries. Leave it there and don't move. You're going to be fine."

She looked up at me with a much clearer expression than before the crash. Her eyes were focused on me but worry creased her forehead. "What happened? Where's Rotna?"

"We crashed on the planet, and the ship is really beat up. In fact, it has split up in at least two pieces. I'm not sure how bad it is yet. Last I heard Rotna was injured but fine." I smiled at her and patted her hand. I didn't know what to say or how to comfort her. I wanted to hug her, but she was not in any position to accept a hug yet.

"Is someone on their way to get us?" Lisa lifted her head and looked around at the devastation.

"No, at least not yet. Since we are ok, we have been put at the bottom of the list. I need to let the doctor know you are awake and see what he wants me to do next. I also need to go and check on the holding cells. Venay thinks the ship broke up around them." I winced as I thought about them, and I truly hoped they all survived this. There would be nothing worse than being abducted by aliens, and then killed in a crash just a week later.

"What? Why? You are the Commander's mate! You should be a priority. Why isn't he doing whatever he can to get you safely to him?" She wrinkled her forehead and pursed her lips.

"Lisa, he has everyone on board to think about. Plus, those aliens crashed too. I don't know how far away they are, but

I'm sure he's working very hard on getting all of the healthy warriors together and see what they have in the way of defensive weapons that still work. He has called me a couple of times. I'm healthy and strong. I can pull my own weight. And what I need to do is make sure you are okay before I go check on the rest of our people. Are you alright with that?" I looked her in the eyes and put on my most courageous face. She needed to know she was in the company of someone who could take good care of her while she was healing.

"Of course, you're right. I'm sorry. My life before this week was pretty ordinary. I never had to deal with anything more than a sprained ankle. My parents are upper-middle class, and I grew up in a nice neighborhood, went to a good school, was a cheerleader," She tried to make a hand gesture as she said cheerleader, but it didn't come off too well. She must be very stiff and sore all over.

Her face contorted a bit before she continued, "You know, the normal life of a happy kid. I never had to take care of myself. In fact, my parents were paying for my condo. They thought I should experience living on my own for a while before settling down and marrying. I had only graduated college a couple years ago. I could afford a cheap apartment in a not so nice area, but my dad didn't want me anywhere near that neighborhood so they bought me a condo." She rattled on and I could tell she was nervous and in pain when she grimaced after each little movement.

"Hey now, why don't you just lay there and rest for a bit, I need to call the doctor and see what he wants next." I got up and walked away to call the doc.

"Paris to Doctor."

"Yes, Paris, how can I help you?"

"I found the med-kit, and it's working on Lisa, thankfully! But she is in a lot of pain. She's awake now, which is good, but I don't think I should move her. Can she stay here by herself for a while? Or do I need to keep an eye on her?" I spoke softly so Lisa couldn't hear me.

"If you give her a pain injector she will sleep, and you can go do what you need to. But don't leave her alone for very long. You were right not to move her. I need you to read me the stats from the healing device on her abdomen."

I read what I could, but some of it didn't make any sense to me.

"Good, good. Do you see the long injector in the kit?" The doctor asked. "It might look like a fat pen to you."

"Yes, I have it," I responded.

"Right, on the side you will see a small dial, I need you to turn it so that is reads 'glozxhen.'"

"Is that the pain medicine?" I asked.

"Yes, do you have it?" He inquired.

"Yes." I turned the dial to the correct medicine and hoped I was doing the right thing.

"Ok you only need to inject it into her arm. Just one push on the button at the top once you have it level with her skin."

I put the pen on her arm and pushed the button. "Okay, that was easy. How long before she starts…"

I looked down at Lisa's face, and it was slowly calming and relaxing. The tension had melted away very quickly, and she was having trouble keeping her eyes open.

"Oh, it's taking effect quickly. I think she might already be asleep." I chuckled.

"Good, but don't be gone longer than an hour. I need you to check her vitals every hour. If the display shows a beeping yellow number, then call me right away," He ordered.

"Okay, will do," I replied.

"Paris, are you going to check on the slaves?" The doctor asked.

I cringed when he used that word. I wished they had a better name for the humans.

"Yes, I know the bridge is most likely cut off from them,

and I'm not too far away." I stood up and took another look at Lisa, hoping she would be just fine all by herself. She looked so tiny laying on the floor in the middle of the storm of junk all around.

"Good, you will want to stop in empty rooms along the way and pick up a few med-kits to take with you. And maybe a few sheets too. I expect you will find some dead but a lot of injured. Call me back when you get there and let me know how you find them." He sounded so matter of fact. I wondered how he wasn't stressed or worried at all. Maybe doctors were just good in a crisis and had learned to turn off their emotions?

"You haven't been able to get anyone there yet?" My voice rose and I had to mentally calm myself to keep from freaking out.

"No, we are close to the bridge and cut off from the back of the ship. If there is an emergency, I will find a way to get there. But for now, you will have to be my medical assistant."

I took a deep breath, "Alright, anything else I need to know?"

"Do your best to turn off your emotions. If you need to stop and take a moment to yourself, do so. But don't take too long."

How does one go about turning off their emotions?

"Got it, alright I'm heading out now. Chat soon." I closed my eyes and took another deep breath trying to shut off my emotions and prepare for what I knew was going to be something so much tougher than I had ever experienced.

To bolster my nerves a bit I repeated my mantra, *I can do this. I am strong and independent. I don't need Venay to rescue me.*

I covered Lisa with a blanket and put a pillow under head. If she woke before I returned, I hoped she wouldn't be too upset with me for knocking her out and leaving her all alone.

The hallway wasn't too bad. Some of the doors were open and items from inside the living quarters were sprawled all over the hall, but it wasn't bad. The mess served as an obstacle course and I had to weave around various items to move forward. I decided to check the open doors first for med-kits and sheets.

At first my arms were full and starting to hurt from carrying so many kits and sheets, then I got the smart idea to use the sheets as a sort of backpack or carrying bag. I took the eight med-kits I found and wrapped them along with the extra sheets into one sheet to make a big bag and slung it over my shoulder. It was heavy and my shoulder hurt, but it was much better than before. I could also get over the debris easier. When I came upon some spots where I needed to climb, I took my pack and tossed it over what I needed to climb on and then had use of both hands.

The sheets acted as pretty good padding for the kits. I could hear the boxes jostling around in my makeshift pack whenever I threw it over a mound, but each time I looked inside the boxes were still closed. If I was lucky, they would all still work just fine when I needed them.

I made it to where the holding cells should have been, but all I found was the end of the ship. It had broken apart right outside the holding cells. That meant that either everyone was on the other side or they were gone.

There was a large gap between my side of the ship and the other side. I saw a lot of debris and what looked to be some bodies, most likely humans since they were wearing Earth clothes.

Tears pricked at the back of my eyes, but I wasn't about to lose it, not yet anyway. I still had to find everyone. Once this day was over, then I could find a small hole and cry my eyes out.

I called out, "Hello, anyone there?"

I heard a response, "Yes, there are a bunch of us still trapped in the cells!"

"Oh, thank the heavens you're alive! Some got out? How? I don't see a way to get to you," I yelled out

"I don't know. Some of the cell doors opened on their own and all the people who could get out did. They left the rest of us here in the locked cells!" It was a woman's voice I didn't recognize.

"Did the men get out?" I yelled.

"Some, but they didn't help, they just ran," Another voice responded.

A third voice spoke up, "That's not true, they went around to all of the cells and pulled on the doors, they ran after checking that they couldn't get us out."

"Okay, I am across the way, but I don't see how to get to you. I'm going to climb down from my side and see if I can find a way to you. Hold on," I yelled.

As I tried to find a way down, I called Venay, "Venay, I'm over at the holding cells. The ship broke up on my side. But I'm climbing down to see if I can find a walkway to them. There are a lot of people still locked in. Some cells unlocked, but not all of them."

"Yes, once we crashed, I pushed the button to let them out. I'm sorry not all of them were able to get out. Be careful, I can't imagine it will be easy to get across the divide. But if you are able, I can guide you to the manual override so you can unlock the rest." His admission surprised me. I would have thought he'd want to keep them in their cells no matter what.

"Wonderful! I think I see a section that might still be somewhat attached. If I can get to it, I won't have to climb all the way down the ship only to climb all the way back up." I breathed a sigh of relief.

"Be careful, Paris, and call me when you get there." He hung up, and I re-focused on my task.

It took me a good thirty minutes to climb to the spot I

saw. It looked like a hallway that had been mangled but still attached to both sides.

I climbed up an embankment and then slid down the other side. It reminded me of those plastic slides kids played on. You would climb up one side of the plastic only to slide down the other, but this was much larger, and sharper. I cut my arm on the way down, but it wasn't too bad. Once I got to the bottom I stopped to clean and bandage my arm.

I didn't take any more time than what I needed. Those people needed me, and I still had to get back to Lisa too. I wouldn't make it back within an hour.

I found a good way to get up, but it must have taken me at least forty-five minutes. I was sweating by the time I made it back up. The path to my right looked like it might be the way to go for the holding cells. Or at least I hoped I was on the right floor, I counted seven floors going down and then seven going back up.

"Hello, are you guys still there?" I yelled out again, just to help me get my bearings.

"Yes, you sound much closer. Are you almost here?" The first lady I was speaking to earlier yelled out.

"Yeah, I'm just down the hall now. But there's a lot of debris, I should be there within a few minutes." As I climbed over some metal piece of the ship, the doctor called me.

"Paris, did you make it back to Lisa? How is she?"

"Sorry doc, I still haven't made it to my people yet. I'm almost to their holding cell. The ship broke up between me and them. You could probably get someone over here to help."

"Why didn't you go back to Lisa?" The doctor sounded worried for the first time.

"Because a lot of the humans were still locked in their cells. When Venay released them only some cell doors opened. Those people took off when they realized they couldn't help.

But Venay told me how to open the cell manually so I'm going to release them and leave them with the med-kits. It should be a faster trip back to Lisa." At least I hoped it would be faster.

"You say they are on our side of the ship?" He asked.

"Yes, I think so, unless the ship broke up into three pieces?" That thought hadn't occurred to me and I really hoped it wasn't the case.

"Something tells me that is what happened. Did you climb all the way down to the ground and then up again?"

"Almost, I found one warped hallway still attached so I went across that, but it was seven stories down and then up again." I was panting from the exertion, but I doubted he even noticed.

"Be careful Paris, the Commander will be very upset if you get injured," The doctor admonished.

"I know. I'm being careful. Okay, I'm here now. I need to let you go. I'll call back if there is something I can't handle myself." My heart rate increased at the thought of finding seriously injured people. Using the back of my hand, I wiped at the perspiration dotting my forehead.

We said goodbye, and I found the panel Venay told me about. He had called me back while I was climbing up and told me where to find the panel. I took off the cover, and there, like he said, was a large lever. I pulled it down and the cells unlocked. I heard a loud click.

So did the people inside as I heard their cheers of joy. Then the bars opened up. I walked into the room and everyone was excited to see me. A few asked if we crashed on Earth.

"We are a long ways from home, crashed on an alien planet controlled by the V'Zenians. But the bad part is that we were fighting an alien ship who had better technology than we do. They are injured as well and followed us down to the planet. I don't know where they are, but we need to get moving somewhere else. Is anyone here injured?" I looked to all the people climbing out of the cells.

"Yes, but this could be good, right? Another alien race could be our rescuers?" Betsy asked. She had a hopeful look on her face that was covered in scratches and dried blood.

I walked over to her and hugged her. "Betsy, I'm so glad to see you're alright. But, these other aliens are worse than our current captors. They are not humanoid like us; they're insectoid. You don't want them catching any of you." I pulled back and examined her closely.

She did look pretty good, but I noticed she was standing on one leg. "Did you hurt your leg?"

"I think it is sprained but not too badly." Betsy winced.

"Ok, sit down while I check you out." I pulled the sheet of supplies towards me and took out one med-kit.

"If any of you have any sort of first aid training, please come over here, and I'll show you how these work. We're going to need every bit of help we can get here." I opened the med kit and pulled out the diagnostic tool.

One woman came over whom I hadn't seen before, "My name is Donna. I'm a pediatric nurse, but I'm sure I can help with the adults too."

"Oh good! Come here while I show you how to use the med-kit's diagnostic tool. The doctor will be happy to know you're part of the group. He can't get here because the ship is broken up into three parts." I looked at the others and no one else stepped forward.

A few of the people near me called out various questions, ones I had no answers to. "Look, I don't know much, I have told you all I know so far. But we have injured here that need our help. Let's focus on fixing them up first, Ok?"

A few grumbled "Okays" made their way back to me.

I showed Nurse Donna how to use the diagnostic tool, but it was going to be hard for her to use since she didn't have a universal translator implanted.

"Does anyone here have a universal translator implanted?" I looked up at those who were still here. Some had snuck out once they were let out of the cages. I couldn't blame them, but they should have stayed and helped.

Two women spoke up and said they did.

"Great, come over here. We're going to need your help." I relaxed knowing I wasn't the only one here who could understand the alien tech.

I showed them how the diagnostic tool worked and then how to fix Betsy's sprain. It was going to take each of the girls with the translators to help others use the equipment. I also handed out some of the supplies so that everyone could help clean up the cuts on most of the people.

Some of the guys were still here too. So I had them lift those who couldn't walk and put them with the others who were injured.

"Ok, do you guys have a handle on it here?" I was antsy to get back to Lisa and check on her.

The nurse said she did, so I left her in charge and also instructed the other two how to make a call on their devices and who to call in case of an emergency.

Betsy looked at me with either fear or trepidation in her eyes; they were wide, and she had tears building in them. "Where are you going? Why aren't you staying with us?"

"Lisa is injured and unconscious. I have to get back to her before she wakes up. She's on the side of the ship where no one else is located. I can't leave her there alone. All of you here need to stick together and once everyone can walk, try to make your way to the front of the ship. The doctor will help you all." I pointed to the general direction of the med-bay.

I heard a few say they would rather try to make a go of it on their own here on this planet than be taken back as slaves. I couldn't disagree with them. So I said nothing more.

CHAPTER FIFTEEN

I made my way back to Lisa. It was slow going but faster on the way back like I thought it would be.

She was still asleep, thankfully. I checked the device on her stomach, and it was healing nicely. It looked like once she woke up she might be able to slowly walk away. I wasn't sure if she would be able to make her way to the med-bay, but she could probably get out of this ship if she had to.

The doctor called me, and I told him what was going on. He was very impressed with what I had done in the holding cells with everyone who was left. Those guys were going to go and check on the others in Bravo cell and see if anyone needed help there.

On my way back, I did try to look for anyone who was in the living quarters, but I never heard anything. Made sense though. They should have all been at some sort of battle station since we had been in a battle. I would have been surprised to see anyone in the living quarters area, besides my people. It dawned on me I hadn't heard from Cazon or Sheila yet.

I tried calling Cazon but couldn't reach him so I tried Sheila.

"Paris, oh thank goodness! I was so worried about you! Where are you?" Sheila's voice broke and I felt awful for forgetting about her.

"I'm with Lisa in her quarters. She was badly injured, and I'm just waiting for her injuries to heal. They have some pretty advanced equipment here. How are you?"

"I'm fine, a bit scraped up and will certainly have some nice bruises, but overall, just fine." She sounded relieved and I knew she was going to be fine.

"How is Cazon? I couldn't reach him," I asked.

"I haven't been able to reach him either. With the power issues maybe his communicator is out?" Sheila sounded optimistic.

"I don't think it works like that, but maybe. I really don't know. Can you get over here? Do you even know how to get here?" I knew if Cazon was conscious he would have called Sheila. But I didn't want to worry her.

"Um, no. Can you come get me?" She asked.

"Sure, what's your cabin number?"

"I don't know. How do I find that out?

"Go outside to your hallway and look at the number to the left of your door." I instructed her.

She gave me her number, and I made my way there. We grabbed her med-kit and a few more as we made our way back to Lisa. I figured if I had to go out again, we might as well have some med-kits with us. I also picked up a couple laser guns and two Taser guns as well. It was best to be prepared. Then at the last minute, I grabbed a few sheets too. I wanted to be able to cover bodies if we came upon any. So far, there were only the three I saw in the holding cell. The guys took care of covering them up for me.

Lisa was still out of it when we got back, so Sheila and I chatted. I told her about everything that had happened today, and she was shocked that I was able to get over to the cells and back safely. "Man, you are one tough chick, Paris. No wonder the Commander wants you." She chuckled and shook her head.

I, on the other hand, started to blush. Compliments weren't something you get when living on the streets, usually it was just the opposite. "Thanks, I had company for a lot of it. You didn't. Looks like you are one brave cookie."

"Nah, I buckled in and just went for the ride. Once it was all over, I started to worry and pace. If you hadn't called me when you did, I would have gone stir crazy and eventually gone out wandering through the ship. I would have done it sooner, but Cazon was very insistent I wait in our cabin until he contacted me." Sheila grinned and I knew she would have done exactly that. It was a good thing I contacted her.

"Well, the three of us are here together, that's what matters now. But I should probably go and check on the people from the cells. See if they are ready to move yet. I would like to get them all over here and spread out amongst the different cabins as much as possible. That is if they don't want to head to the med-bay. But something tells me that most of them will leave the ship, and to be honest, I won't blame them if they do." I shrugged, knowing the planet would be difficult to survive, but if I didn't have such a strong desire to get back to Earth, I'd probably join them. Anyone who ran from the ship would never get back to Earth.

"You still stuck on the whole save the slaves thing?" Sheila asked.

"Of course, aren't you?" A little indignation entered my voice, but I didn't care.

"Yes, but to a point. Cazon is a great man, and I want him. I don't need to go home. But then again, I'm also the one who has fantasized for years about meeting a hot alien man who would make me fall in love with him." She laughed and grabbed her stomach and leaned over flinching in pain.

"Sheila, are you ok?" I grabbed one of the other med-kits

and took out the scanning device and moved her hands out of the way so I could scan her stomach.

"Well, according to this machine, you have some mild internal bleeding. I need you to lay down so I can put the tablet on and heal your stomach. I doubt it will take long, but I don't know how much blood you have lost either." I shook my head and realized I really should have done a better job checking her over when I found her.

She followed my orders, and I had that device on her stomach. We chatted until Lisa woke up.

"Hey," Lisa said groggily.

I looked over to her, "Hey there, sleepy head. How do you feel?"

"Tired, and sore. I think I might be a bit hungry too. Do you think the replicators are online?" Lisa being hungry was a good sign, I hoped.

"Doubtful, but we do have some protein bars. I'll go grab you one and check your vitals." I left the room to find the food.

Sheila and Lisa chatted while I went to the kitchen.

While I was in there I decided to call Venay, since I hadn't heard from him in a few hours. "Venay, what's going on?"

"Paris, are you still in Lisa's room?" he asked.

"Yes."

"Good, stay there. We have seen signs of the Insectoids nearby. I think some of the slaves got out and have been captured by them. There were a few areas that our scouts said looked like a fight had broken out. Then they also saw insectoid foot prints walking away. We have surmised that the Zateelians have captured our humans and are carrying them off somewhere." Venay's voice was tired and sad. Even though they were his slaves, I knew he wanted to keep them safe.

"No, no no. It's all my fault." Panic took over and I paced the small room.

Venay interrupted me. "Shh, calm down. It's not your fault. This is on the Zateelians, not any of us."

I had to make him understand. "I released all of the people in the jails and left them. I had to get back to Lisa and told them I would come back and check on them. Many were injured and one of the non-injured is a nurse, so I showed her and a couple others how to use the med-kits. I need to get them to come here with the injured. We have plenty of empty rooms around us. Maybe we can even make some sort of a defensive position and fight off any insectoids?" I rambled on worried about the rest of the humans.

"No, it's too dangerous. The sun looks to be setting soon, and they like the dark. I am sure they will be back and looking for more humans to take. Stay where you are and find a way to lock yourselves in. I wish I could be there with you, but I know you will do great." Venay paused and sighed. I could hear the stress coming through his voice. "Have you seen anyone else?"

There was no way he could get to me. Not with the way the ship was in pieces. Plus, he was in charge and needed to be on the bridge, or wherever he was running everything from.

"Yes, I found Sheila and brought her back here too. So it is the three of us. Have you heard anything from Cazon? Sheila can't reach him, and neither can I." I rubbed my neck as the aches and pains from the crash were starting to come back in force.

"Sadly, I haven't. I have to assume he was badly injured, and either can't get to us or can't move," He huffed. It sounded like Venay was angry, but without seeing his face I couldn't be sure what he was feeling. I didn't know him well enough to be able to tell his emotions just from his voice.

"No, I don't buy that. I know he's going to be fine, maybe there's just an issue with his communicator. He could have hit his head and damaged it." Cazon had quickly become my friend. I wouldn't believe he was seriously hurt until there was proof.

"Yes, that is possible." I could hear the uncertainty in his voice. He didn't believe my excuse but was going along with it to appease me.

Losing Cazon would be hard. He was my only friend amongst the aliens, well, besides Venay. Sheila was falling for him, and it would be tougher on her. I decided not to tell her anything, and let her think there was hope until we knew for sure.

"Sheila and I scavenged some weapons and med-kits on our way back to Lisa's place. But I didn't think to get food. Is there any way to get these replicators back on line?" My stomach gurgled as I thought about food.

"Not at this point there isn't. Try the rooms next to you, see if there are any rations in those kitchens. And if you find any more weapons, grab them. But don't go too far." Venay's voice softened and I heard a door close behind him. He must have power where he is, or he manually closed the door so we could have some privacy to speak.

"Alright, um… are we going to be stuck here alone on this side of the ship all night?" I knew I sounded like a baby, but I didn't care. The other aliens were out there, and they had already taken some of the humans with them. I only hoped Venay was lying about the Zateelians and they would take good care of them.

"No, I am going to send some of my warriors to get you three, and if they can get the slaves on the way back, even better. But if they do find you, make sure you bring all of the med-kits, weapons, and rations you can carry. We are going to need them." His voice was firm. There was no way he was going to let me stay the night all alone.

It made me feel all warm and fuzzy. I knew he had so much on his plate, as did all of the warriors. Sending a team to get us probably wasn't the smartest thing to do with his resources, but it made my heart swell for him.

"You got it. I'll go scavenge some more now while it's still light." I could hear the hope in my voice and knew we were going to be alright.

"You have lights in your hallway?" Venay asked, sounding hopeful.

"There are some emergency lights on, and then the big hole in the ship has leant us some natural light as well. I'm not that far from it."

"Good, with you being so far up from the ground, you are farther from where the enemy will start looking for any survivors. So stay on your floor. Lock your door and block it with any furniture you can once you finish scavenging the rooms around you. But, don't leave your floor." Now he was sounding like the Commander again, ordering me to stay safe.

"I'll be strong and get us all through this, but Venay, I really miss you."

"Oh sweetheart, I love hearing you say that. I miss you too. If I wasn't the Commander I would have come to get you as soon as we landed. I am sorry I haven't been able to come get you yet. The next set of warriors to come in, I will send them to you." His soft voice gave me comfort and I knew I'd see him soon.

"Venay, you should probably get the other humans first. They're closer to you than I am. And I have no idea if the injured have anyone to look after them right now. My guess is that most have taken off, deciding it would be safer to hide out on the planet. That's what I would have done. Well, I would have made sure that everyone went with me. I wouldn't have left anyone behind, unless they wanted to stay." If the Zateelians were out there, and if they really were the true bad guys, it looked as though something had finally gone right for me. I was in a much better place than the rest of my species.

The humans who were lower to the ground, and exposed to the planet, were in a lot more danger than I was. Plus, I had a communicator as well as weapons and most likely some protein bars or whatever they kept in the kitchens for emergency rations. I doubted those who found a way out of the ship had anything but the clothes on their backs.

He chuckled, and it was nice to hear him laugh, even if it was just a simple chuckle. I started to feel warm and knew that we were going to be just fine.

"Paris, I love you, and you come before the slaves. My men will get you first, then they will look for the slaves. I want you here with me. Besides, it sounds like the doctor could use your help more than any of my warriors." He chuckled again. I wish I could have been there to see his smile. "The few who have the required first aid training are nothing but trouble, according to the doctor. He told me what you did for Lisa. He is very impressed; she would have died if you hadn't done such a good job."

"Okay, enough praise for one day. Get back to work so that your next set of warriors can come and get us. And if I hear anything, I will be calling you right away." I felt very uncomfortable being praised for doing what any human would have done in my shoes. I didn't deserve it.

"You better, but if you hear something, be as quiet as you can. And shoot anything that comes through your door," He ordered.

"Yes, sir!" We said goodbye, and I continued looking for food in Lisa's kitchen. I brought everything back I could find.

Both girls were awake and hungry, which was a good sign.

I checked the device on Sheila's stomach, and it was ready to come off.

"Thank you, Paris! I'm so glad you know how to work

that thing. Now give me a protein bar." I wasn't sure if she was joking or hangry, I went with the former.

I laughed and handed her a bar.

Once she took a few bites she smiled and appeared content. I hated to tell her any of the news. I was actually surprised that Venay told me so much. But I guess since we were here alone with no one to protect us, he needed me to know what was going on so we took the situation more seriously, and so that I would obey his orders. If those insectoid things were out there, I wasn't going anywhere just yet. He must know enough about me to know that I would have gone after all of those people in the cells and brought them back here, if it wasn't so dangerous.

"Okay, I spoke to Venay." I took a seat on the floor near both girls. "He suggested I scavenge the surrounding rooms and get all of the food. We're going to be here for a few more hours, but once his warriors get here, we will need to bring back supplies with us. They don't have a lot and everyone is making their way towards the bridge and med-bay. We could really help them out if we have a nice big haul of rations and med-kits."

Sheila started to get up, "Sheila," I put my hand on her shoulder, "Stop. You can't go with me yet. I need you to stay here and keep an eye on Lisa and to also protect her in case anything gets in here that shouldn't." I raised my eyebrows at her hoping she would get the idea.

"Oh, of course. I can do that. Is there anything else I can do while I wait for you?" She sat back down and eyed me.

"No, you should rest. It looks like your internal bleeding is all fixed, but I don't want you to re-open any wounds. We should all get some rest while we wait for the troops to rescue us." I laughed at that thought. "Like we are damsels in distress or something." Sheila joined me in the laugh, however short lived it was. But it did help to relieve a bit of stress.

I spent the next hour going through the rooms and bringing stuff back. I also set up the dresser in front of the bedroom doorway. It would make a good wall to hide behind if the aliens made it this far.

One of the last rooms I searched was more of a supply closet, and in it were some weapons, ration packs, more med kits with bandages and cleaning supplies-things we could probably really use in bulk. But I also found a couple of night vision goggles, or at least that's what I thought they were. I put the lenses over my eyes, and I could see everything in green, but in better detail.

When I went back into the hall, it was darker. It seemed that the emergency lighting had dimmed. I looked down toward the hole in the ship and it was a lot darker, as though the sun was setting. It was possible that there were a lot of holes in the ship and some of what I thought was emergency lights were pinhole lights from outside.

I put the night vision goggles on as I made my way back to the room. This was going to be my last haul for now. I needed a break, and I wanted to go check something out before all of the light was gone.

Once I had dropped the stash in the room near the girls I asked, "Sheila, you good here? I want to go check one last thing before we hunker down for the night."

"Sure, what did you see?"

"It's getting dark, and I found these goggles that I think will help me see in the distance, at night. I want to try to see what is around us. There's a hole in the ship not far from here and we are pretty high up, so I might get an idea of what's around us." I had taken the goggles off before entering Lisa's quarters, so I brought them up and showed Lisa and Sheila.

"Is it safe? I mean if those insectoid aliens are anywhere near here, won't they see you?" Lisa asked.

"I doubt they will see me up high like we are, in the dark.

But I might be able to see them. I brought a pair for you too. If it gets too dark, put them on if you hear any noise so you can see what it is. When I come back, I'll knock three times quick and two times slow, like this." I demonstrated my knock for her. I wanted to make sure she knew it was me and didn't shoot me when I came back.

"But Sheila, if I'm not back within an hour, you have to assume something happened and stay here. Don't go anywhere. Call Venay and let him know what happened. alright?" I put my hand on my friends' shoulder and smiled.

"Paris, if it's dangerous why are you going?" Sheila was a bit of an adventure seeker, but I hoped she would stay with Lisa and take care of our friend. There was no one else in this part of the ship to do so.

"Danger is my middle name. Didn't I ever tell you that?" I smirked at her and walked off without another word. I did close the front door, in hopes that the aliens wouldn't be able to open it. All I took with me was one power bar, a water bottle, two laser guns, a Taser, and the night vision goggles. I didn't plan on being gone long, but after all of my experiences, I have learned to pack for the worst.

CHAPTER SIXTEEN

I quickly made my way to the edge of the ship, where I had climbed down earlier to get across to the other side. Just before I turned the corner to the drop off I heard screaming. I stopped at the corner and slowly angled my head around to see what was going on. I saw what I guessed where the insectoids. They had found some humans and were grabbing them and taking them away from the ship.

These things were called insectoid for a reason. They looked to be a cross between a giant, mutant cockroach and a grasshopper. They were taller than I expected, about my height. They were either camouflaged, or they just had the same coloring as the trees all over the outer parts of the ship. They were various shades of green with bits of brown on the edges. It wasn't quite dark yet, but with the night vision goggles, I could see pretty well at a distance. They were bipedal, but that was the only thing that we appeared to have in common.

This was going to be a problem. I was covered in goosebumps. It was really difficult getting their image out of my head. On the one hand, I wanted to step on them and squash them like the bugs they were, but on the other- giant, mutant, cockroaches! Gross!

While I was trying to pull myself together, I heard a chorus of gut-wrenching screams and looked back around the corner and almost puked. One of the insectoids had bitten off the head of one of the men. As I watched, his dead body fell in a heap at the feet of our real enemy.

They were definitely not here to help us. Venay had been right.

I heard a cacophony of chittering. They sounded like a swarm of grasshoppers making noise and I wondered what they were saying. My universal translator wasn't helping. Was there a way to translate bug into English?

Before I pulled out my laser gun, I shook my body trying to get rid of the heebie jeebies, and then I looked to see if I could get a good aim. I counted thirteen of them, and they were corralling more than a dozen people down the side of the ship and towards a giant hole that led outside.

I needed to make sure my people wouldn't get shot in the process. It was a mix of men and women who were their prisoners. I didn't recognize any of them but that didn't matter, they were my people, and I was going to do whatever I had to in order to protect them.

So far, I had a good aim on several of those giant bugs. However, to get the rest I would need all their prisoners to drop to the ground … or run away.

I decided to risk it, and I took aim and fired on the one closest to me. It was a direct hit! The humans did what I assumed they would naturally do, and they dropped to the ground. A few in the back of the group did try to get further back inside the ship, out of my range, which was a good thing.

Another bug went down with my next shot, and after my third one, they knew where I was at and pulled their weapons and started shooting at me. One of them got close, his laser shot hit the wall next to me and sparks flew toward me but with those goggles on, my eyes were protected from the sparks, just not from the glare. I had to back up and take off the goggles and rub my eyes a few times before my vision cleared up.

However, I had the high ground, and they were in a bottle neck, for the most part. I shot a couple more, and then the cavalry showed up. My guess is they were the ones who were coming for me.

They were on the other side of the chasm from me, and they started firing at the mutant bugs from their side, I counted five warriors. Hope blossomed in my chest as I realized we had a real chance to beat these things.

One of the humans went down, but it looked like a mutant cockroach hit her with its arm, hand? Not sure what their appendages were called. But she went down hard, so I aimed for that thing above her and hit it dead on its chest. It wasn't moving again.

While I was shooting at the remaining bugs, I received a call from Venay, "Paris, what in the universe are you doing? I thought we agreed you would stay inside with Lisa and Sheila and wait for my warriors to get you?"

"Kinda busy now. I'll call you back when the bad guys are all dead." I hung up not waiting to hear his reply.

I went back to focusing on killing those suckers, and it looked like the warriors had finished them off for me. A strange feeling came over me, and I was mad. *How dare they take my kills?*

I probably had bloodlust. As I considered what I felt, I realized I wanted to be the one who killed them all, or at least the last of them. Anger was bubbling to the surface of my emotions, and I didn't like it one bit. I should have been happy, or even grateful for the assist. Instead, I was livid that I wasn't the one who finished them off. What a weird feeling. That came out of nowhere.

Could it be some sort of PTSD from everything that's happened? I wasn't sure what had caused me to go crazy like I did, but I didn't like it. I had to get control of my feelings before anyone found me.

I stood up and shook my hands out and paced the hallway, taking deep breaths.

Once I felt more in control, I called Venay back, "Sorry about that. I found these night vision goggles when scavenging, and I only wanted to try them out. I had no idea I would find those mutant cockroaches hurting my people. Once I saw what they were doing, I couldn't help it. I started killing them, and then your warriors showed up and finished them off." I knew I was rambling, but I couldn't help it. I felt tears start to fall down my face and I did everything I could to keep from balling while communicating with Venay.

"I can't believe you! What am I going to do with you?" For the first time since the crash, he sounded angry with me.

I sniffed and chastised myself when his tone changed. "Paris, are you hurt? What's wrong?"

"I'm fine. It's been a very long day and my emotions are getting the better of me. I'm sorry. I don't mean to be a crybaby." I ran a hand across my face and wiped the tears away.

"Oh, sweetheart. Crying is totally normal. You are so brave. I can't imagine how it felt to go through everything you have today. I should have sent someone to get you sooner. Can you forgive me?" The strain in his voice was evident when his voice broke on the last sentence. "What can I do to help you get through this?"

"Train me?" I shrugged my shoulders and smiled, even though I knew he couldn't see what I was doing.

"I guess I will have to if you keep this up." He sighed, "Paris, are you really okay? They didn't hit you, did they?"

"No, they didn't. I'm just fine. Now that your warriors are here, I'll go and get Lisa and Sheila, and we can all go back with my people as well." I felt as though a load had been lifted off my shoulders when it sank in that we were being rescued by the good guys.

"Alright, I will contact Zelan and let him know to expect you three. Do you need any help?" He asked.

"I could probably use one warrior. The rest should stay there and protect the people. There were at least a dozen of them, and one was hurt in the fighting. And another …" My voice broke when I thought about the one who didn't make it.

His voice softened. "Okay, wait where you are, and I will send one warrior to help you."

"Great…" I was cut off when out of nowhere a huge bug came at me with its pinchers. Up close it looked like it had pinchers.

I moved back to get out of its reach, but it had a long range. It grabbed my arm, and I was forced to drop the weapon I was holding. But I had another gun in my pocket, and using my free arm, I grabbed it quickly and tried to shoot it, but his other arm knocked it away from me.

It was pinching my arm so tightly that it broke skin, and my arm was bleeding. I screamed out loud and tried to kick the thing in what would normally be a man's softest spot, but it didn't do anything to the mutant in front of me.

Venay was yelling into my communication device, but I couldn't focus on him. A warrior from across the chasm yelled at me to duck. I did the best I could and he shot at the bug as it was going to punch me in the face. Thankfully I ducked just in time. Its pincher hit the wall behind my head and the laser shot hit it in the neck.

Its head hit the wall, and I grabbed the Taser I had in my pocket and shot it. That released its hold on me. And I backed up and grabbed one of my guns on the floor and shot it in its chest. If that didn't kill it, I was in trouble. But it fell back to the ground and stopped moving.

The warrior yelled across the divide, "Back up. I see another one climbing towards you."

I did as commanded, and I saw three warriors shoot at the floor right below me. I heard a high pitched squeak or squeal, not sure what it was. But it hurt my ears. And then a thump as it fell to the ground.

Venay was still yelling at me. "Venay, I'm fine. My right arm might need some help, but other than that I'm fine."

"What happened?" He was breathing heavily, almost like he was running.

"A couple of the bugs crawled up to my location. One got a hold of me, they are really strong. I had no idea what it would be like to fight them. And kicking them in the crotch does nothing! Where are their reproductive organs located?" My mind was focused on finding my new enemies weak spots, so I knew exactly where to hit them next time.

He laughed, and what a welcome sound that was. "So you are really alright, besides your arm?"

"Yes, I'm waiting here until a warrior climbs up. I'm sooo not walking back to Lisa's without an armed escort." I looked at my arm and realized I was going to have to clean my wound and probably would need some antibiotics.

"Good, make sure you keep your eyes and ears open. They make a clicking noise when they get close to you, so pay attention. I am almost to the holding cells so I will see you soon."

"Venay, stay on the bridge, I'm fine." I couldn't believe he had gotten here so fast. He must have already been close by when the bugs attacked me.

"No, Paris, I am not taking any more chances with you. Besides, sounds like you have a lot of humans you might need some help with." He had already planned on helping us. Something inside of my chest loosened a bit thinking about how he had taken the time to come and help humans, who he called slaves.

"Okay, thank you, Venay! I can't wait to see you."

We ended our talk while I waited for the warrior to get to me. As he made his way up each level, he took the time to check the surrounding area, which turned out to be a good thing as one of those monsters was lying in wait for him. But the warrior, who I learned later was none other than Zelan himself, was a very tough pureblood. He heard the thing or sensed it or something because he pulled his weapon out and was aiming for it before the cockroach knew what hit him.

I had been leaning over the side watching his ascent when I noticed him take his weapon out and shoot. How all of those bugs got so close to me, I will never know. The only thing I can think is that they were a scouting party and were already on their way to my side of the ship.

He got to the top and asked, "Paris, are you alright?"

"Yes, I am. Thank you." I reached out and grabbed a piece of cloth from the ground and used it to wrap my injured arm.

"Let me take a look. Do you have a med-kit with you?" Zelan reached out for my arm.

"No, I didn't think to bring one." I raised my hand to his.

"No problem, we can find one on our way back to your quarters." He helped me up from the ground and kept a hand on my arm.

We found a med kit in the first room we checked, and he used it to clean my wound, and then put some gook on it that seemed to seal the cuts in my arm. It also had some sort of numbing agent as the pain went away, and I couldn't really feel my right bicep any longer.

"Don't try using your right arm for at least an hour. If you do, you could break open the wounds. It is just a sealant used in the field to help get you to the doctor so he can sew your arm up properly." Zelan inspected his work and started to put the supplies back into the kit.

"Can't you use that square device in the med-kit that

looks like a tablet? Wouldn't that seal my arm up?" I pointed to the device with my left hand.

"Yes, but you can't move while it is working. We don't have time to sit down and wait. It is very important that we hurry up and get your friends and get back to the other side of the ship." He had the kit in his hand and reached out with his other one to help me up from the chair I had been sitting in.

"Oh, yea, I guess there could be more bugs here huh?" I don't know why I thought we had time to waste healing me up properly. I didn't want to meet any more Zateelians. All I wanted was to cuddle up next to Venay and take a very long nap.

"Yes, and I don't feel like fighting with three injured females in my company." Zelan raised an eyebrow.

I chuckled, "I guess I deserved that. But you must admit I did pretty good, all things considered." I puffed up my chest with pride and stood a bit taller as I thought about what I had accomplished so far today.

"Yes, for a civilian human you did really well. Now let's get moving." He led me out of the cabin and back toward my friends.

It didn't take us long at all to get Lisa and Sheila, along with all the stuff we scavenged. Zelan had a very large back-pack which he used to haul most of our stuff. He gave me one to wear, and it was as full as I could handle. Granted, that wasn't as much as he could handle, but I did my part.

He made a comment that he was going to have to send some teams back during the day to scavenge for more food, weapons, and med-kits. We would need it all.

"Zelan, how far are we from the settlement on this planet? Why haven't they come to get us yet?" I wasn't sure how long it had been, but certainly over eight hours.

"They don't have ships that can easily fly here. They have one space ship, but it is more of a cargo ship. They are a small settlement and don't have many warriors with them. There haven't been any issues for this planet in decades. But I can see that we are going to have to change that way of thinking." Zelan stayed in the lead and his head moved around looking at every corner and shadow.

"That still doesn't explain why they haven't come to help us." I narrowed my eyes at his back.

"We are a long way from them, and using their land transports, it will take them several days to get here. But, we have asked them to stay put for now."

"Why? We could use their help." I was astonished that we weren't asking for their help.

"Because they have children in their compound. It is more important that they protect their families. We aren't sure what the Zateelians are up to. The Commander felt that we could make our way there easier and safer than if they tried coming to us. But we won't have to wait long. There are a couple of ships on their way here. I wouldn't be surprised if they made it here in two or three days' time. It would be much safer for the settlement to stay put and defend itself and their children." Zelan sounded so matter of fact, like we just hadn't been attacked by insectoids who could eat a human.

"Yeah, I can see how that would be a problem. Divide and conquer and all that. Why are these bugs attacking you guys? I don't get it. Venay told me that your two species had an agreement of sorts." My head began pounding and my arm started to ache again.

We kept walking and had made it to the end of our section of the ship. All chatting stopped while we surveyed our surroundings and decided which way to go down.

"Paris, I want you to take the rear. I will take the lead, and when I say to follow, I want first Lisa and then Sheila to climb down to my level. Then you will come last. I need you to pay close attention and have your laser pistol ready at all times. Can you handle that?" He looked me directly in the eye.

"Yes, sir, I can." I nodded.

"Alright, I am going to go down to the next level, but wait until I give you the all clear before you come down. Paris, keep an eye behind us, in case any of the enemy troops have already made it to this level." Zelan made his way to the first level while two of the warriors were across the way keeping watch on our path.

Once we all made it to the lower floor, Zelan went again to the next floor. We almost made it all the way without any issues.

CHAPTER SEVENTEEN

I was getting ready to climb down to the level with the semi-bridge that went across to the other part of the ship when I heard a clicking noise. My night vision goggles were around my neck so I put them on really quickly, as the sun had already set, and we were operating mostly by starlight. I couldn't see a moon yet, but I also didn't know if there was a moon orbiting this planet.

I could see a slight movement down the hallway. "Paris to Zelan"

"Zelan here, what's the holdup?"

"I hear something, and I see some movement close by. Keep an eye out for bugs." The clicking noise had me on edge and while I was ready to fight for our lives, I really hoped I didn't have to.

"I am going to term our comm and call to the warriors across the way to get a light shining on your floor." Zelan ended our comm before I could reply.

I took off my night vision goggles so I wouldn't lose my sight. Right after I took them off, I sensed something close by. I pulled them back up to my eyes, but I couldn't see anything in front of me.

But I felt something along my leg. I looked down to the floor and discovered those stupid bugs could crawl. I aimed my laser gun at its back and fired. It grabbed my ankle and pulled me down on the ground. I fell with a hard thump and knew I was going to be sore.

My one shot didn't do much damage to its back, but once I was down on the ground it tried to crawl on top of me, and I was able to shoot its head. Note to self, next time I shoot a big mutant bug that is on top of me, close my eyes and mouth. Its head burst and got goo all over me and in my mouth! That wasn't coming out anytime soon.

Before I had a chance to even think about what happened, much less throw up, more bugs came at me.

I heard some more scuttling, but the warriors across the way had their light shining and yelled at me to stay down. They started shooting and hit two more bugs.

"Yeah, sure no problem. I can get this bug carcass off all by myself," I grumbled. It was tough, those things were heavy, but I got it off. Then I laid there trying to clean my face off and listening for more clicking or scuttling sounds.

There were none, so I stood up and looked down the hall but couldn't see anything. I quickly ran to the edge of the floor and made my way down to where Zelan was.

"Hey, you ok?" He looked at me and checked my limbs. Then he looked at my arm that was injured from earlier.

"Wonderful, one more reason for the Commander to yell at me. I should have gone with my gut and brought another warrior with me so he could take up the rear guard instead of you." He shook his head and let out a long, deep breath. "We are going to have to clean this wound and rebandage it, but I want to get across to the other warriors where we will be safer."

"I am shocked that experience didn't make you sick. You are much tougher than I imagined a human woman would be." Zelan was actually paying me a compliment.

"Well, my last five years has brought much worse than a cockroach spewing on me." I looked down and noticed blood was running down my shoe onto the ground.

"Zelan, my leg is bleeding. Should I clean it before crossing? Will they be able to pick up my blood trail?"

"Possibly, stay right here. I will send the other two across and come back to help you. But keep your pistol pointed down the hallway." Before walking away, he called to the other warriors across the way to make sure they kept their light pointed down the hall and stayed alert.

"Ok, thanks." I kept my eyes down the hallway while he helped my friends to cross the warped bridge. He came back with a med-kit and pulled up my left leg to check it out.

"Great, another wound for the Doctor to sew back up. The Commander is going to kill me." He sighed and shook his head while he cleaned my wound. Then he put that numbing gel on it and wrapped it up tight. He tore the bottom of my pants away so that I didn't have any more blood dripping on the ground.

"Stand up. Can you walk?" He asked.

I stood up and bounced on my legs a couple times, "Sure, it seems fine."

"Alright, let's get moving. You take the front, and I will cover our rear." Apparently, he had decided if bugs attacked from behind, he would be the one to battle with them.

We made our way across the divide with no more issues.

I was only two more levels away from the top when I heard a commotion above us. It was Venay yelling at the warriors. It sounded like he thought I should have already been up there.

I yelled out, "Venay, I'm almost there. And I'm fine. Be right up."

He couldn't wait, so he met me at the next level, grabbed me in his arms, and hugged me so tight I could hardly breathe. "Venay…can't…breathe."

He put me back down on the ground and started to kiss me, "What is that smell and taste?"

"Oh, well, I uh… I was attacked on our way over here, and I had to shoot a bug in the head while it was close to mine." I shrugged. "We wanted to wait until we got up here before I cleaned off and changed clothes. Plus, I forgot to bring a change of clothes with me."

"Let's get you to the doctor for an exam, and then we can clean you up. How do you feel? Where are you hurt?" Venay's voice was rigid and no longer held the emotion it had only a few seconds before.

"I have two injuries, one on my right arm and the other on my left leg. But I'm fine. Zelan patched me up, so I'll be good until the doc can look me over. I would prefer to clean up first though. Is there anywhere here I can do that?" I looked around at where we were, and there did look to be some crew quarters here, but I wasn't sure.

"I would feel better if the doctor examined you first. He is waiting on the other side. If you feel ok, we should hurry up and get moving so he can check you out first." He turned his head and began to walk away.

"I think Lisa and Sheila are hurt worse than I am. He should look at them first." I began to wonder why he was so worried about me getting checked out. I only had a few cuts, it wasn't anything major. Was it just because he wasn't used to feeling so strongly for a woman?

"They won't make it there as fast as we will, so you will be first. Let's move." He didn't wait for me. Venay took off so fast I almost had to jog to catch up to him.

We made good time because as soon as we got up to the right floor, he picked me up and carried me as fast as he could go to the doctor. We did have some more climbing to do, which he let me down for, but for the most part it was a quick and easy ride for me. I was just so happy to be in his arms that I didn't complain about being carried. For the past few hours I had wondered if I would see him again. So, letting him carry me was my reward for surviving the day.

Back on Earth, I would treat myself to something nice each time I made it through something that may have seriously hurt or killed me. It was never anything big. One time I fought off two big guys who were hurting a dog, which was how I ended up with Lola. She was my treat that time. I missed Lola and wondered how she was doing. I had made a few friends who helped me to care for her. Maybe one of them was caring for Lola now?

I had to shake myself out of those memories. Earth was no more for me. Today was what I needed to focus on. When we made it to the front section of the ship, I saw a sight for sore eyes. There was a giant hybrid, he was almost as tall as Venay, waiting on the other side of a beam that had fallen. He had a huge smile on his face to go with his compassionate eyes. The doctor was waiting for us.

"Paris, it is so good to see you alive and well. I understand you were injured, please tell me what happened." The doctor's eyes took in my situation and he held out a hand to help me over the beam.

As I began to explain what happened and where I was injured, he took out a diagnostic tool and started to scan me. He was listening to me but just barely. That is until I got to the part about shooting a giant bug that was crawling on me. He took his diagnostic tool and scanned my head right away and breathed a sigh of relief.

The doctor looked at Venay and said, "She is clean." Everyone around us breathed a heavy sigh and smiled.

"Um, what does that mean? I am clean?" I wasn't clean. I was disgusting with bug goo on me. Not to mention all the dirt and grime from the crash.

The doctor patted my uninjured arm, "It just means you have no head injuries, dear. But I suppose you are quite dirty.

Why don't you come with me, and we will get you all cleaned up?"

"Ok." I followed the doctor, and Venay followed me. "Venay, don't you need to get to the bridge or something?"

"No, I am not leaving your side until this is over. I will stay with you in the med-bay until the doctor says you may leave, and then you will come to the bridge with me. You are not leaving my side until we are all safe and this planet has been eradicated of those Insectoids. They are too dangerous to leave, and you are not going to be near them again." The sharp tone in his voice worried me. There was definitely more going on than anyone was saying.

"Oookaaayyyy." I drawled out as I rolled my eyes, "overprotective much" I mumbled to myself.

"Yes, yes, I am. I almost lost you today, and I won't go through that again." Venay ran a shaky hand through his hair and looked pleadingly at me.

The doctor spoke up, "Paris, for the sake of the crew, will you please do as he asks? He has been a zylan since he heard you were first injured. Please don't torture the crew any more by letting him loose, all alone, alright?" He patted my shoulder again, and I could only laugh.

I looked at him, tilted my head, and squinted my eyes, "What's a zylan?"

Venay responded, "It is like your bears, but much more ferocious. The Doctor is implying that I have been attacking my own warriors today." He looked over at the doctor who cowered a bit and grunted.

"Alright, fine. I would prefer to be with him anyway. But I don't want to get in the way of his job. I know how important it is that he stays focused." Inside, I was actually yelling and jumping for joy.

While I didn't want to disturb his work, I also knew I would be happier near him. It was the strangest thing. All I could think of was the stress of the ship crashing and then the multiple attacks from the Zateelians had me acting like a silly girl. I was stronger than this and I had never needed a man to take care of me before. But I had never been through something this traumatic, not even when I lost my parents.

"Trust me dear, he won't be able to focus without you now." The doctor took me by the hand and led me to a bed in the med-bay. He conducted some more tests and cleaned my injuries and used their advanced medical technology to close up my wounds.

"Through those doors." He pointed to the side of the room, "Is a shower that is working, for now. Please take a shower and I will send in some clean clothes for you to wear."

Venay tried to follow me into the shower, "Oh buddy, you can stop right there. I will be totally safe in the shower all alone. Please wait outside." He looked me up and down, chuckled, and turned to walk out of the room.

I took a long shower, the water was warm and it felt so good to wash my entire body with soap and hot water. I had to wash my hair three times to make sure I got all of the alien insectoid goop out of it. My mouth was another matter. I used the body soap to clean my mouth out, it did *not* taste good. However, it was better tasting than the insectoid brains I had in my mouth. Just thinking about it made me shiver, even in a hot shower.

When I stepped out of my shower, there on the cabinet, were some clean clothes and shoes. They all fit quite well, which was rather surprising. I asked Venay, and he informed me had someone grab some clothes for me earlier in the day. He had always planned on keeping me close to him and had stocked his personal office with items just for me.

Another chink in the armor around my heart broke. If I wasn't careful, I'd be in love with the giant alien before long.

CHAPTER EIGHTEEN

The next couple of days flew by. I never left the bridge unless Venay was with me, but I was kept busy. He turned his office, which is where we slept, into a small triage center. The doctor was so impressed with my field work that he asked Venay to let me help him. Venay had no issues with me helping as long as I stayed on the bridge or in his office. So the doctor set up a triage center there.

If a warrior or human could make it to me, then I could treat them. He sent the nurse from the holding cells over to help me as well. We made a good team.

After so many years on the street with no one to trust, it felt nice to be part of something bigger than just me.

"Doctor to Paris."

"Yes, doctor? How can I help you?"

"I need you to get your friends out of my med-bay! They are in my way and are keeping my patients awake when they should be sleeping," A frazzled doctor pleaded with me.

"Well, you could tell them that I need their help and send them my way. If that doesn't work, I'll call them myself." I smiled thinking about the girls and what they may have been up to.

About an hour later both Lisa and Sheila showed up, looking a bit unhappy with me. Lisa asked, "Why do you need our help? We aren't medics. We can't help you. We should be in the med-bay with Rotna and Cazon, not here with you." Lisa crossed her arms over her chest and actually hmph'd. I almost started to laugh.

The day we crashed, Cazon was found unconscious and taken to the doctor. He had broken his leg and sustained some internal injuries, but the doc patched him up. Since then, he's been stuck in the med-bay.

Rotna was also stuck in the med-bay. I had heard they would both be released soon, but wasn't sure what the doctor meant by *soon*.

"For starters, I can use your help organizing things here. But, more importantly, you need to not spend so much time in the med-bay. You're in the way of the doctor and his nurses. Also, as I understand it, you have been, um..." I looked down at my hands, this was awkward. "Stimulating your men when they should be keeping their heart rates down and getting some sleep."

Sheila spoke up, "No, we have not been stimulating them. Only lying in bed and kissing them. That is all. Neither of us would do more than that in front of the entire med-bay." She shook her head as though I was the crazy one.

"Ok, but you need to understand that those guys need rest, not kissing. Please only visit as long as the doctor allows, or you might be kicked out for good. I don't want that to happen. And besides, I really could use your help here. You don't have to be a medic to help." I pointed to the stack of supplies that needed to be organized and inventoried.

Lisa and Sheila exchanged glances, "I guess you are the Commander's mate after all, aren't you?" asked Sheila.

I laughed and moved on to the next patient.

"Venay, how many people have we recovered?" I asked him.

"Only 132 of the 200 we started with." He looked up from the tablet he held in his hands. I could tell Venay wasn't happy with the recovery numbers.

"That isn't good. If you combine that with the 36 who have died, we are still missing 32 people." I wondered where they were and if they were okay.

Venay tried to console me, "I am sure most of those 32 are fine. They have probably gotten far away from here and are safe now. They will most likely live out the rest of their lives here on this planet."

"I wish we knew for certain, and if they are out there all alone, I still want to find them. If they want to stay here that's fine. But I want to know that they're alright." I walked over to him and put my arm around him and rested my head on his chest. He wrapped his big, strong arms around me and kissed my head.

"I am sorry, Paris, but we have to wait until we are certain we have killed all of those bugs. I like your term for them." His chest rumbled with his laugh.

We both looked into each other's eyes and smiled. He was about to lean down and kiss me, but his second in command cleared his throat.

"Yes, Eereen, what is it?" Venay was a bit cold in his response, but Eereen did seem to have impeccable timing when it came to interrupting our kisses on the bridge. We probably shouldn't do that.

"We have an incoming message from the fleet, Commander." Eereen bowed his head and moved away.

"It's about time. They should have been here yesterday." Venay moved to a console and pushed a few buttons. I couldn't hear what the other person was saying, but I could hear Venay's side of the conversation.

The expression on Venay's face changed from being

almost pleasant to outright rage. "They WHAT?" I hadn't seen this side of him before. He was waving his hands all over the place while yelling into the communicator on the bridge. "No, I am not upset with you, I am downright angry with the Zateelians for attacking us like this. They basically declared war upon us. Attacking my ship was one thing, but then to have two space cruisers here waiting for you, *that* is war!"

This was bad. Really, really bad. It looked like we might be here for a while.

"Have you destroyed their ships Captain?" I could hear Venay clearly, but I couldn't hear the other person talking. So I inched closer in order to see if I could hear what he was saying.

If I focused hard, I could hear him. It sounded like they were still fighting, but since the V'Zenians brought three ships, they were winning the battle. One of the enemy ships was destroyed, but the other one was putting up a bigger fight.

"No, we have no way to repair this ship as it is, and our weapons need power in order to work. There is nothing we can do from here to help you. If one of your ships is too badly damaged to help you, send them here to our location. We could use the manpower down here to finish off the insectoids who crashed with us." Venay's shoulders relaxed a bit and he stood up breathing in and out in an effort to calm himself. This was something I had seen him do several times and wondered if he had an anger management issue.

I thought I heard the Captain agree, but I wasn't sure. As I tried to get closer, Eereen noticed me and shook his head. I hung my head and stepped back a few paces. Venay would tell me later.

I was right too. Later that night as we were readying for bed, he told me what happened in space these past two days.

"We should expect to have company tomorrow. The third

ship in this system is badly damaged, and if they can land, they will come over here to our location, and then we will have enough troops to find and squash those bugs. But I must warn you, they are hardened warriors who see humans as either mates or slaves. They won't understand how I have treated our current residents. They will expect me to hand them over to them to keep locked up, that is if their holding cells can handle the numbers."

"You can't let them. Most of those who stuck it out here have been helping. And they want to stay on this planet and try to make a go of it here if they can't go home. Why can't we let them do that?" Frustration was setting in and I was in no mood to teach another ship of aliens that humans were not their slaves.

"It isn't my law or my rules. I won't have a choice if the other captain demands it. We can't keep them here in this ship. Most likely we will all go over there, and I will be subject to their leader, as long as he is ranked a Commander or above. If we are equal rank, he retains command since it is his ship." He shrugged as though he had no control of the situation and would accept whatever came.

"What else could he be if he isn't a Commander?" I sat up against the wall and looked at Venay standing in front of the wash basin and wondered if there just might be a chance of Venay staying in charge.

"If he is a new ship captain, his rank might be Captain. After Captain is Commander. You usually make Commander after three to five years as a Captain. Some make it somewhere between two and four years. But if he is only a Captain, and even if we are on his ship, I will take command. He and his crew will have to follow my orders." Venay moved toward our make-shift bed on the floor.

Since we moved in here, we have slept together, but nothing more than kissing was taking place. He hadn't even tried anything, which was a good thing. I wasn't ready to marry him, and I certainly wasn't ready for anything more intimate than a kiss.

"Then let's pray that he is only a Captain. It would be nice to have a real room again. I can't say I will miss sleeping in your office." I snuggled down next to him and tried to go to sleep. We had the best accommodations at the moment. Everyone else slept wherever they could find a place to lie down.

CHAPTER NINETEEN

The next day saw the arrival of the new ship. It made a safe landing a few miles away from us during the day, and we set off in groups of twenty to fifty. Larger groups held the injured and included some of the humans. Venay and I were in the last group. He said the Commander of a ship always goes last, and since I was not to leave his side, I was last as well.

Surprisingly, we all made it safely to the other ship. I wondered if the Insectoids knew we had too large of a contingent of warriors for them to mess with. Or, if they were just biding their time.

When we entered the other ship, there was a line of all of the senior officers waiting for us. The current ship's Captain, and he was only a Captain, was waiting to welcome us officially and to hand over control to Venay. I didn't realize how much I was dreading this moment until I came face to face with the being who was to be the new second in command. My smile must have been a mile wide because Venay nudged me with his shoulder and cleared his throat.

"Captain, I would like to introduce you to my mate. Paris, this is Captain Montgomery."

I put my hand out to shake the Captain's hand, "Captain, it is nice to meet you."

He took my hand but. instead of shaking it, he kissed it much like a gentleman on Earth would do. "The pleasure is all mine, ma'am."

I tilted my head to one side and smiled back at him and had to work hard to keep from sighing. What a nice surprise. Not that I was attracted to him, but meeting a gentleman way out here in the middle of a battle with mutant insects was very nice.

Venay looked at me and arched an eyebrow; he would be asking me about that later I was sure.

"Let me show you to your new quarters. We will be here a few months while we work on the repairs we can. Fleet will send some ships along with a garrison of warriors to encamp here going forward. But our engineer doesn't think this ship will fly until we get the supplies in about five months' time." Captain Montgomery led the way.

"Five months, we are all going to stay here for five months?" I looked up to Venay with questioning eyes, and I bit my lower lip to keep from saying anything else.

"It depends on what happens with the two ships in orbit right now. If one of them goes home then we will go with them. This is not my ship so it would not be right for me to stay here if there was a way for me to go home and get a new ship to continue my missions." Venay linked his hands behind his back and followed the Captain.

"Oh." What could I say? He wanted to keep abducting humans, and I couldn't say anything negative in front of Captain Montgomery. I just realized that I was going to have to be very careful with what I said in mixed company.

Once we were in our new room, which just happened to be the Captain's quarters, I heaved a heavy sigh and plunged down on the couch. "Venay, does this mean that we can be officially mated now? There are plenty of troops here to take care of the issue with the vermin population. Can we have our honeymoon?" Over the past few days I learned that I had in fact, succumbed to the pull of the mating bond.

I wasn't sure if I was ready to tell him I loved him, but I was ready to take that next step in our relationship, if for no other reason than to ensure my position as the mate of the Commander. With this new group of warriors, I knew my position was tenuous and I would have to be on my toes all the time until Venay claimed me, officially.

He came over and sat next to me, "We could, but don't you want to wait until we can honeymoon away from here? We can't leave until all of the Insectoids are dead."

"I know, but we could have our ceremony now, couldn't we? You could take a day off, and we could stay here in our room together? With no one to disturb us? There is an able bodied Captain who I am sure wouldn't mind staying leader of this crew for one more day." I looked up at him with a coy smile and wrapped my arms around his neck, then I bit my lip while considering what to do next.

He took that as an opportunity to kiss me. As he leaned down, he took my lower lip between his and sucked on it just enough to get my teeth to release it to him. I kissed him harder and leaned against his chest and heard a moan coming from his throat. "Yes, I think we could manage that. How about tomorrow if nothing else gets in the way?" Before I could answer, he kissed me again and again.

It seemed like forever until he let me up for air. "Yes, tomorrow would be perfect." I stood up and went to the kitchen to see what I could make us for a late dinner, and try to calm myself. The entire time I was in there I couldn't shake the smile from my face.

It looked as though I had succumbed to Stockholm Syndrome and didn't care in the least bit.

EPILOGUE

Our mating ceremony was very similar to a marriage ceremony on Earth, but without all of the pomp and circumstance. And no formal attire. Venay assured me this was very normal since so many humans mated with the V'Zenian warriors on the way back home, to their home that is.

We spent the night all alone with no disruptions. It was perfect. We stayed in bed the next day too. But the day after that he had to go and attend to his duties. I was sad to see him go, and I think he was as well.

"Paris, as soon as we are certain the insectoids are all taken care of, we will go away for a week, just the two of us." He kissed the tip of my nose and I sighed.

"Perfect! Go and kill 'em all!"

If you want to read the next book in my series, *Worlds Collide*, and find out what happens next in the series go to the link on my website: Worlds Collide

Keep reading to get the first two chapters in Worlds Collide.

Do you remember Natalie from early on in this book? She becomes our main character in this next adventure. I can't wait for you to get to know her better!

Reviews are the life-blood of an author, would you take just a minute to leave a review of *Worlds Away* wherever you purchased this book from, I would be forever grateful.

You can also leave a review and follow me on BookBub. https://www.bookbub.com/authors/j-l-hendricks if you follow me, you'll get updates when I send out a new book. BookBub is the gold standard of book promotions! They have almost 9 million readers! All indie authors aspire to get a BookBub promotion! The more followers I have on Book-bub, the better my chances of getting a deal with them are. So, help an author out and leave a review?

I hope you enjoyed my PG-13 version of a sci-fi alien abduction adventure/romance. The adventure parts of these books have always been my favorite, so I thought why not make a clean version for everyone to read.

The story will continue, and we will see them all on the alien planet at the beginning of the next book. Another couple will become the center of the story, but we haven't seen the last of Paris and Venay.

If you want to read more of the worlds I have created, check out these other places:

Blog/website: https://jlhendricksauthor.com/blog/ here is where I'll do new cover releases and even share snippets of my upcoming books! So be sure to subscribe. You can also see all of the books I've written to date and find the links to get them.

Twitter: https://twitter.com/TinkFan25

Facebook: https://www.facebook.com/JLHendricksAuthor/

Keep an eye out on my blog or social media accounts for news about other books I have coming!

But the best way to stay up to date on what I am doing,

and the next book release, is to join my mailing list. https://jlhendricksauthor.com/newsletter/

I'll even send you a free book, or two, just for signing up for my newsletter!

In fact, if you sign up, you'll get a special prequel to the Worlds Away series, Worlds Revealed. It's all about the true story of Roswell!

ACKNOWLEDGMENTS

I say this every time, but it really does take a lot of people to put a book together!

Beta readers are very important! I only had three this time, Leo Roars, Rebecca Reddell (author friend who rocks!), and Dawnya Goode, but they picked out some things that needed tweaking as well as some of the spelling errors I missed, thank you all so much!!!

Book covers are the most important aspect of creating a book that readers will pick up. I found a pre-made cover on SelfPubBookCovers that was just awesome!

My author group, 20BooksTo50K are the best group of authors anyone could want! They are always so supportive and engaging! Thank you guys from the bottom of my heart!!! In fact, Rebecca Reddell from my group helped me immensely with further character development and my issue with commas! LOL

For those who didn't know, this version of Worlds Away is very similar to the original, but I did go back and make a few tweaks to some sentences and fixed some grammar and spelling issues I missed earlier. This new version has about 6,000 words more than the last one did.

Keep reading for the sneak peek of Worlds Collide!

Book 3: The Emerald Portal

<u>Mr. Clause series coming Christmas 2021</u>

See these titles and more at https://www.jlhendricksauthor.com/

The enemy of my enemy ...

All Natalie wants is to save the other humans from the aliens who abducted them. Then, she discovers something even worse than the V'Zenians. When their ship crash lands on an alien outpost controlled by her keepers, after the battle in space with the Zateelians, she begins to think the only way to survive is to work with those who abducted her.

Zelan is a V'Zenian warrior who's never agreed with the policy of abducting humans. When he finds himself face to face with his worst enemy, he realizes how much he respects and admires the spirit and tenacity of the humans aboard his ship. He fights tooth and nail to protect them and destroy the enemy hellbent on infesting them all.

The Zateelians crashed on the outpost as well and are after the humans for something very different than slavery. All the humans and V'Zenians on the planet will make for a smorgasbord of action for them.

If you enjoy clean alien romance, then you will love Worlds Collide!

This is a very good series with characters you like and want good things to happen to and an enemy that is horrible and you want them squashed like the cockroach they look like. - Amazon Reviewer

PART I
WORLDS COLLIDE

CHAPTER ONE

"Natalie, you are with me today. We need to scour the back section of the ship for supplies while we wait for the Star Prime to arrive." Zelan pointed to me as I sat in the cramped corner of the room I had been staying in since the Zamaya crashed.

Those of us who were too stupid to get away once the ship crashed had all been corralled and brought to the front of the ship. We were all split up into different rooms and sections. Some even had to sleep in the corridor. I didn't know many of the women in this section because most of them had been in the other room of abductees. The aliens called that room Beta, and ours was called Alpha. They were so original with their names. However, I was making friends.

I missed Paris and Sheila, two of the women I met after being abducted by the huge, alpha aliens. They had become my friends. Zelan told me Paris was really busy with her assignment as a medic. I didn't know she had a medical background. I had thought she was homeless. Maybe living on the streets gave her a quick medical background?

"Where are we going today? And please tell me you guys

have killed all of those giant insects. I don't think I can take another one touching me, even if you do kill it. That stuff they discharge when you kill them takes forever to come out and stinks something awful!"

Yesterday, when we were out scavenging the ship, we came across three insectoids inside our ship who were ravaging our supplies. They were stuffing their backpack shaped bags with medical supplies as well as with our food bars. I thought that their ship must have taken a lot of damage for them to come over here during the day. Zelan thought they had been here all night and were waiting for the sun to set before setting off back to their ship.

The mutant insectoids, the Zateelians, who invaded our ship after shooting it down from space, didn't like the sunlight. They could stand to be outside for a little while, but not too long. It is thought that the sun hurts their eyes. The rest of their body seems to be very strong. I know this because it took three shots from Zelan to kill one of them who had me pinned down on the ground. It slathered some goo on me, into my face to be precise, and then was backing away. My guess is it knew that the next shot was going to kill it, and it did. This then put more of that slime on my body. I couldn't win, even when they died. After that, we went straight to the med-bay where the doctor examined me and proclaimed me clean.

What was that all about?

I was covered in that disgusting, viscous discharge the bug left all over the top half of my body. I was NOT clean. However, everyone around me seemed to breathe out at once, like they had all been holding their breath. I needed a twenty-minute shower to get all of that slime off but was only given ten minutes. I swear my hair still smelled of mutant cockroach slime.

Today should have been about me resting and recovering, I still had a bump on my head from when that creature attacked me and caused me to fall back to the hard ground. I couldn't sleep all night thinking about the creature that almost ate me. Now Zelan wants me to go back out with him again?

Is he crazy?

CHAPTER TWO

"Great! Out of one jail cell and into another. Natalie, I thought that we were done with that? Why can't the Commander let us stay in rooms instead of forcing us in here?" Betsy asked me as we were herded like cattle into our new "accommodations," as the new captain called them.

Accommodations? Yeah right!

The *Star Prime* arrived today. We had been sent over to the other ship. While it was damaged in the space battle with the Zateelians, it made its way to the planet mostly unscathed. It was in much better shape than our ship. So it was decided that we all needed to head over there.

Betsy had wrapped her arms around her middle section, and I could see she was holding back tears. We had spent the past couple of days on Commander Venay's ship and helped them to round up supplies and even take care of the wounded. Paris was really in her element acting as a medic on the bridge with the Commander watching her every move. We deserved better treatment than this.

"Betsy, I don't know. Maybe we can ask Paris when we see her next. If things go back to the way they were, then I bet she will bring us our meals again." I tried to offer her a smile, but I didn't think it came out very well.

"Natalie, these cells are even smaller than the other ones. How are we going to spend 5 months cooped up here while we wait for our abductors to bring in a new ship?" Betsy had been complaining non-stop since we made our way to the new ship.

But I couldn't fault her for it, I wasn't much better.

The ship we were on originally, had been broken up into three pieces after we crash landed on this alien world.

"I wish I knew." I huffed out and looked up to the ceiling. My right hand automatically made its way to my forehead while my left one tried to rest on my hip. This was what I did whenever I was nervous or stressed out. We were so tightly squished in here that my elbow hit someone else on their back, "Sorry about that." So I dropped my arms to my sides in silent misery.

The new male warriors served our evening meal. I didn't recognize any of them from my time on Commander Venay's ship. They must be from our new prison ship, the *Star Prime*. It was that stupid, chalky, jello garbage that we had when we were first abducted. "Hey, why are you feeding us this garbage? Where is Paris? She used to bring us Earth food." I asked one of the new warriors on guard duty.

"This is standard fare for slaves. Be happy that you are getting anything at all," he stated with zero emotion in his voice. He sounded more like an android than a person. But then again, this was a regular soldier who was accustomed to fighting and picking out slaves. Not one of the slave trade warriors who made regular trips to Earth, and therefore was comfortable with us.

Over the past week, we had started to make quasi-friend-ships with a few of the warriors who guarded us on a regular basis. Somehow, I doubted these new guys would become our friends.

"Can I ask where Paris is?" If I could talk with her, maybe we could get better food and accommodations.

"She is spending time with the Commander. They are to be mated tomorrow," Mr. Personality said.

"Really? Already? Isn't it a bit soon?" My jaw dropped as my hands flew in the air and bounced down on my thighs, hitting someone in the process. I mumbled an apology, but she didn't even register I'd hit her.

"No, it is not. If this is what they want, then now is the perfect time. Our Captain can take good care of this ship without the Commander." He sounded like he wasn't too happy with the Commander taking over.

"Oh, I see how it is. You don't like the Commander, do you?" I eyed him up and down as he squirmed before answering me.

"There is nothing wrong with the Commander. I just do not know him. But it is safer for his mate to go through with the ceremony. Once that happens, no one on this ship will touch her. She will be treated like a queen. You might want to consider your options as well. Spending the next five months in these packed cells will not be pleasant." He spun on his heels, walked over to the next cell, and ignored my requests to get a message to Paris.

"Hmph, maybe Sheila or Lisa will come visit us tomorrow, Betsy." I narrowed my eyes at that guard and decided that he was definitely not going to be the warrior I would mate with, if I ever did.

The next morning Zelan was part of the group who brought us our breakfast. I never thought I would be happy to see him, but I was. "Zelan, is there any way to get better food on this ship? Seriously, even the ration bars would be better than this stuff." I scooped some up with my spoon and let it drop back onto my plate in white, sticky, globs. I didn't know how much longer my stomach would allow this as sustenance before it revolted.

"Natalie, their food replicators do not have recipes for Earth food. This is all the lead warrior will allow us to bring you." He dropped his head and then looked back up at me. "Unless, would you agree to be my mate? I could protect you better that way, and you could find more palatable food."

"Um, thank you, but...I," I tried to shuffle my feet, but there was very little room while most of the women in my cell sat down. "I am still hoping to go home to my fiancé. I thought that we might somehow make it off this planet and back to Earth." I couldn't look him in the eye. I knew he had an attraction for me; he must have since he chose me every day to go out with him and scavenge the old ship.

"I am sorry, but you will never make it back to Earth. I hope you realize that soon and start thinking about a future with me." He moved off to the next cell of women and gave them their breakfast. All I could hear was soft "ugh's" and "not again" as the warriors fed the rest of my prison mates. Normally they chatted with us. I had guessed that things on this ship were going to be a whole lot different than before. And sadly, I was right.

There was no way I was going to become a mate to some alien who had abducted me from my perfect life back home. Well, okay it wasn't perfect. But it was my life! One I wanted so desperately to have back.

UNTITLED

Doesn't that sound like a blast? Come on over to my website and pick up your copy today! Or, check the online retailer where you picked up Worlds Away to see if they are selling Worlds Collide! Find out what happens on the planet with Natalie and the other human women.

Worlds Collide!Do they exterminate the Insectoids? Or do the insectoids thrive on this planet?

How will Natalie let go of her past and look to her future?

Also, don't miss out on all of the books in this series!

Worlds Revealed

Is book 0 and a novella set on Earth during the Roswell incident! Venay's Grandfather tells us his version of the epic events as no one on Earth really knows what truly happened! (currently only available to those who join my newsletter)

Worlds Explode

Is book 2.5 and a novella set on Zeleron 10. It is best read after you finish book 2.

Worlds Entwined

Is book 3 and takes us back to Earth! Soooo much is going on in this book! You won't want to miss what happens!

NEWSLETTER SIGN-UP

By signing up for my newsletter, you will get a free copy of the prequel to the Triple J Ranch series, Finding Love in Montana. As well as another free book from J.L. Hendricks.

If you want to make sure you hear about the latest and greatest, sign up for my newsletter at: Subscribe to Jenna Hendricks' newsletter. I will only send out a few e-mails a month. I'll do cover reveals, snippets of new books, and give-aways or promos in the newsletter, some of which will only be available to newsletter subscribers. You'll also get a heads-up when I'm running sales on my books!

JennaHendricks.com/newsletter/

JENNA HENDRICKS
TRIPLE J RANCH
Finding Love
in
Montana
A Triple J Ranch Prequel

CONTACT THE AUTHOR

For those of you who love social media, here are the various ways to follow or contact me:

BookBub: https://www.bookbub.com/authors/jenna-hendricks

Instagram: https://www.instagram.com/j.l.hendricks/

Facebook: https://www.facebook.com/people/JL-Hendricks/100011419945971

Website: https://jennahendricks.com

www.ingramcontent.com/pod-product-compliance
Lightning Source LLC
Chambersburg PA
CBHW030917060726
47591CB00005B/1580